Restoring Faith

Tara Baisden

STERLING RIDGE PRESS LLC

Copyright

Cover designed by Sterling Ridge Press LLC

Published by: Sterling Ridge Press, LLC www.sterlingridgepress.com

ISBN: 978-1-966093-03-9 Printed in the United States of America

First Edition: February 2025

For permissions, contact: tara@tarabaisden.com or visit www.tarabaisden.com

Contents

Dedication

To the builders—
The ones who construct hope out of heartbreak,
Who turn cracks into character,
And who see beauty in what others might discard.

This book is for the dreamers who refuse to give up,
The faithful who cling to grace,
And the romantics, who believe that love—divine and human—can
heal even the deepest wounds.

And to you, dear reader—
Thank you for picking up this story. May it remind you that restoration is always possible, and that sometimes, the most beautiful things
are built from broken pieces.

Chapter 1

Faith McNeil knew three things with absolute certainty: wood never lied, numbers didn't make excuses, and no one could be trusted with her heart. At least, that's what she'd learned in her thirty-two years of life, and those lessons had served her well enough so far.

The early morning sunlight streamed through the windows of McNeil Construction, casting long shadows across her latest project, a hand-carved mantelpiece that would be the centerpiece of the Rogers' home renovation. Faith ran her callused fingers along the grain of the cherry wood, feeling for imperfections. The wood was honest in a way people rarely were, showing its true nature in every knot and whorl.

"You're here early. Again." Monica White's voice cut through the quiet, carrying equal measures of affection and exasperation.

Faith didn't look up from her work, but her lips curved into a slight smile. "Good morning to you, too."

"Good morning to you as well, sunshine," Monica countered, setting a Styrofoam coffee cup on Faith's workbench. "Some of us actually sleep past sunrise, you know."

"Sleep is overrated." Faith glanced up at her best friend and office manager, taking in Monica's silk blouse, pencil skirt, and knowing smile. Her dark wavy hair was perfectly styled, and her bright smile carried its usual warmth, along with a hint of concern that Faith pretended not to notice. "Besides, someone has to keep this place running."

"And someone has to keep you running," Monica said, tapping her own cup of coffee.

Faith's smile widened as she reached for the coffee. "This is why I keep you around."

"Please. You keep me around because I'm the only one who can make sense of your filing system." Monica said, perched on a nearby stool, somehow managing to look elegant despite the sawdust that immediately clung to her skirt. Her dark eyes taking in the organized chaos of Faith's workspace. "The Rogers' mantelpiece?"

"Final touches before installation next week." Faith stepped back, studying the intricate vine pattern she'd been carving. "Their daughter's getting married in three months, and Mrs. Rogers wants everything perfect for the bridal shower."

"Everything you do is perfect," Monica said, then held up a hand when Faith started to protest. "Don't argue. I've seen you redo entire sections because the grain pattern wasn't exactly right."

"Details matter." Faith set down her chisel, brushing sawdust from her worn work jeans.

The sharp trill of her phone cut through the workshop. Faith's stomach tightened when she saw the caller ID: Mercy Regional Medical Center.

Monica's expression shifted from teasing to concerned. "Take it. I'll start getting everything ready for the morning briefing."

Faith nodded gratefully, already lifting the phone to her ear. "Faith McNeil speaking."

"Ms. McNeil, this is Dr. Benson's office." The nurse's voice was professionally warm. "I'm calling about your father's test results."

Faith's free hand curled around the edge of her workbench, anchoring herself. "Go ahead."

"Dr. Benson would like to adjust your father's medication. His latest readings show his blood pressure isn't as controlled as we'd like. She's also recommending an additional stress test next week."

"More tests?" Faith closed her eyes, mental calculations already running. Between the hospital bills and the business expenses... "Is it urgent?"

"Dr. Benson believes it's crucial to keep a close eye on his condition. Considering the seriousness of his cardiomyopathy—"

"Do you have any idea when he might be able to come home?" Faith asked.

"I'm sorry, Faith, but not yet. Dr. Benson feels it's best to continue monitoring your father closely."

"How serious is it, exactly? I mean... what should we be preparing for?" Faith asked.

The nurse hesitated, a brief pause that felt heavier than any words she might say. "At this point, it's hard to predict. His condition is stable for now, but cardiomyopathy can be unpredictable. Dr. Benson will go over everything in detail with you, which is another reason I'm calling." There was a practiced gentleness in her tone, but no amount of sugar-coating could mask the gravity behind her words. "Would you be able to come in tomorrow morning at ten to speak with Dr. Benson?"

Faith's grip tightened on the workbench, her knuckles whitening. "I'll be there," she said.

"Thank you, Ms. McNeil. Please don't hesitate to call if you have any questions."

Faith ended the call and let the phone drop onto the bench beside her. The rhythmic hum of the shop's ventilation system filled the silence, but it did little to soothe the tightness coiled in her chest. She hadn't realized Monica was still nearby until she set a steadying hand on her shoulder.

"Bad news?" Monica asked softly.

Faith shook her head, exhaling sharply through her nose. "No, not bad. Not yet, anyway. Just... more waiting. More bills. More 'what ifs.'" She brushed her palm across her jeans again, a nervous habit she'd had since childhood. "They're adjusting his meds. More tests."

Monica squeezed her shoulder, her gaze steady. "You've handled everything so far, Faith. You'll get through this, too."

Faith gave her a small nod of thanks but didn't trust herself to speak. Instead, she picked up the chisel again, her fingers curling around it as if it were the only thing holding her upright. The motion was automatic, instinctual—a return to the one thing she could control. Wood may have its surprises, but at least it didn't throw curveballs that could irrevocably alter the course of her life.

"I know you don't want to talk about it," Monica continued, her voice carefully level, "but have you thought about not taking on any more jobs for a little while? Ease the workload on yourself. Or maybe even take some time off?"

Faith laughed dryly, the sound almost bitter. "Out of the question, Monica. I need to stay busy."

"Faith..."

Faith shook her head. "Just let it be for now, Monica."

"Will you at least think about it?"

Faith set the chisel down carefully, her hands trembling. "I will," she said.

Monica's lips pressed into a thin line, but she didn't push. She knew from years of friendship that when Faith had made up her mind, there was no breaking through to her.

"I'll be in the front if you need anything," Monica said over her shoulder.

"I know," Faith replied, her voice softer now. She watched her friend go, the sound of her heels clicking on the workshop floor fading into the distance.

If only life's problems could be solved as easily as woodworking—measure twice, cut once, sand away the rough edges until everything fit perfectly.

But life wasn't a piece of wood. It was messy and unpredictable, full of splinters that caught you when you least expected them. Like mothers who walked away without a backward glance, leaving fourteen-year-old daughters to pick up the pieces. Or fathers who worked themselves to exhaustion, trying to hold everything together with determination and pride.

The buzz of her phone pulled her from her thoughts. A text from Monica: "Staff meeting in 10. Donuts included. The good ones from Martha's."

Faith smiled despite herself. Monica knew her too well—knew that in moments like this, Faith needed space to process, but not so much that she got lost in her own head. It was why their friendship worked, even if Faith sometimes felt guilty about how much she relied on Monica's steady presence.

Gathering her papers and tablet, Faith headed toward the main office. The workshop had always been her sanctuary, but duty called.

McNeil Construction wouldn't run itself, and with her father in and out of the hospital, everything fell to her now.

Walking down the hall, she took a moment to look at the framed photos lining the hallway, three generations of McNeil's building and renovating homes. Her grandfather's weathered face smiled out from the earliest pictures, then her father's younger self, and finally Faith herself, the first woman to carry on the family legacy.

She paused at a photo from her first solo project: a sprawling back deck she'd built for their own home. Her father stood beside her in the picture, his arm around her shoulders, both of them grinning at the camera. She'd been nineteen then, so eager to prove herself, to show that being a female didn't make her any less capable.

Now, thirteen years later, she had more than proven herself. McNeil Construction was respected throughout the region, known for quality work and attention to detail. But some days, like today, the weight of that reputation felt heavier than any lumber she'd ever carried.

The main office buzzed with morning activity as Faith entered. Tom Davidson, their senior foreman, was already sorting through the day's work orders. Young Sadie Hatcher, their newest apprentice, practically bounced in her seat, reminding Faith of herself at that age—before life had taught her the cost of enthusiasm.

"Morning, boss," Tom called out, his gruff voice carrying a note of respect that had been hard won over the years. "Got the supplier quotes for the Madison project."

Faith nodded, sliding into her usual seat at the head of the conference table. "We'll review them after the briefing." Her gaze swept the room, taking in her team—good people, skilled workers, all depending on her to keep the business running smoothly.

Monica breezed in last, computer tablet in one hand and a donut box from the diner in the other. She set both on the table with a flourish. "Alright, people, let's make this meeting count."

As Monica began running through the day's schedule, Faith found her mind drifting to the stack of bills waiting in her office. Medical expenses, payroll, material costs—the numbers danced behind her eyes, a complicated choreography she had to get exactly right. One misstep, and everything her family had built, could come tumbling down.

Her phone buzzed again: another text, this time from Mark Winslow at the bank. "Need to discuss the Madison project financing. Can you meet today?"

Faith typed a quick affirmative, even as her stomach clenched. The Madison project was exactly the kind of high-profile work they needed right now, a complete historic renovation that could keep part of her crew busy for months. But the materials alone would stretch their credit line thin, and with her father's mounting medical bills...

"Faith?" Monica's voice cut through her thoughts. "The Rogers' timeline?"

"Right." Faith straightened, pushing her worries aside. Later. She'd worry about it all later. "Mrs. Rogers wants the mantelpiece installed by next Wednesday. Tom, I'll need you and Mike on that. The carved sections are delicate—"

"I'll handle it personally," Tom assured her, making a note in his battered work journal.

Faith nodded, grateful for his reliability. "Sadie, you'll shadow them on the installation. Pay attention to how they handle the finished pieces. There's an art to—"

The office door swung open, and Pete Harrison, the local building inspector, stuck his head in. "Morning, folks. Faith got a minute? A new project needs your attention."

"We're just wrapping up," Monica answered before Faith could speak. "She's all yours in five."

As the meeting dispersed, Faith gathered her papers, already mentally shifting gears. Another project. Another challenge. Another chance to prove that she could handle it all.

But as she followed Pete to her office, Faith couldn't shake the feeling that something was about to change. Maybe it was the way the morning light caught the dust motes in the air, or how the floorboards creaked under her work boots—familiar sounds and sights that suddenly felt different, as if the world was holding its breath, waiting for something she couldn't yet see.

Faith squared her shoulders and pushed the feeling aside. Change was just another word for uncertainty, and uncertainty was a luxury she couldn't afford. She had a business to run, a father to care for, and a legacy to protect.

Whatever came next, she would handle it the way she handled everything else: with steady hands, a clear head, and her heart safely locked away where nothing and no one could reach it.

Just like always.

Chapter 2

Ryan Dalton's GPS chirped its final "destination ahead" just as his truck lurched over a pothole on Main Street. Some things in Laurel Ridge never changed, including craters masquerading as road damage that had been wreaking havoc on suspensions since his high school days.

He downshifted, carefully maneuvering the truck and attached camper trailer through downtown. The same brick buildings lined the street, though some storefronts had changed hands. Martha's Diner still anchored the corner, its neon "OPEN" sign flickering in the late afternoon shadows. The sight triggered a sudden craving for Martha's legendary apple pie, but that would have to wait.

His phone buzzed against the dashboard mount. His mother's face appeared on the screen. Ryan smiled, knowing exactly what she'd say. "Are you sure about this, honey? The university could still use another economics professor."

He let it go to voicemail. He'd call her back once he was settled—or at least as settled as one could be, living in a camper while renovating a farmhouse. His mother meant well, but she and his father didn't understand why their MBA-wielding son had walked away from a seven-figure salary to restore his grandparents' home. How could he explain that some equations couldn't be balanced on a spreadsheet?

Outside of town, he turned onto the maple-lined drive leading to the Dalton farmhouse. The late afternoon sun painted long shadows across his grandparents' former home, its weathered white clapboard siding gleaming in the spring light. Five years of neglect showed in the overgrown yard, gardens, and peeling paint, but the old farmhouse still stood proud against the backdrop of West Virginia mountains, just as it had for years now.

He switched off the engine, and the peace and quiet of the area settled around him. The same peace and serenity he'd known as a child, broken only by birdsong and the whisper of wind through maple leaves. The same peace and quiet he had experienced every time he visited this home, which was often as a child.

He had lived on the other side of town with his mother and father before he went to college and then moved to Chicago. Yet, it was this home in front of him, this sprawling farmhouse that had once been his grandparents, that held the dearest, most cherished memories of his youth. How many times had he turned down this driveway in his imagination during those endless days behind his desk in Chicago? Now here he was, trading spreadsheets for power tools, corporate mergers for morning glory vines.

"Well, Grandma Eleanor," he said, "I finally made it home."

The words caught in his throat. Even after five years, the loss of his grandmother still ached like a bruise. She'd left him the farmhouse in her will, a gift he'd been too caught up in his corporate climbing to properly honor. Until now.

Ryan grabbed his tablet from the passenger seat and pulled up his meticulously crafted checklist. The same organizational skills that had made him a stellar financial analyst now channeled into project timelines and material costs. Twelve months to transform a neglected farmhouse into a bed-and-breakfast. His former colleagues would've called it impossible. His grandfather would've called it a good start.

Grabbing the tape measure, one given to him by his grandfather, Ryan stepped out of the truck. The spring breeze was alive with the delicate fragrance of wild honeysuckle, mingling with the crisp, invigorating aroma of mountain air, so refreshingly different from the artificial sterility of the climate-controlled office he'd left behind.

The ancient porch steps creaked under his weight, a sound that transported him instantly to childhood summers spent helping his grandfather repair loose boards and wobbly railings. Frank Dalton had never met a problem he couldn't fix with enough patience and the right tools. Ryan, thankfully, had been taught some of that practical knowledge.

He fished the old brass key from his pocket, the same key his grandparents had used for decades, and fitted it into the lock. He had to jiggle the key a little before it turned. The door opened with a groan of protest, releasing a wave of musty air and memories. Dust motes danced in shafts of light filtering through the grimy windows. The foyer's hardwood floors, hidden under years of dust, still showed hints of their original glory. To his right, the formal parlor waited behind closed pocket doors. To his left, the library that had been his grandparent's sanctuary stood empty except for built-in bookcases and a stone fireplace.

"Not too bad," he said aloud, his voice echoing slightly in the empty space. The hardwood floors were scuffed but solid. The original wainscoting still held its quiet dignity. Even the plaster walls, though desperately in need of fresh paint, showed only minor cracks. The house had good bones, as his grandmother used to say.

Ryan set his tablet on the central staircase's newel post and pulled out the tape measure from his pocket. The worn metal case of the tape measure was scratched and dented, each mark a story of lessons learned at his grandfather's side. Some measurements couldn't be trusted to laser levels and smartphone apps.

"Measure twice, cut once," he muttered, his grandfather's favorite saying becoming his own mantra.

The library's dimensions matched the original blueprints he'd ordered from the county records department here in Fayette County, but the reality of its condition hit harder in person. Water damage stained one corner of the ceiling. The fireplace brick needed repointing. The built-in bookcases, while structurally sound, would need extensive restoration.

Ryan moved through the first floor, mental calculations and half-formed plans swirling in his mind. The formal parlor could become a cozy sitting room for guests. The library, with its built-in shelves and bay window, would make a perfect office. He could already picture visitors gathered around a large farmhouse table in the formal dining room, morning light streaming in as they enjoyed fresh coffee and homemade muffins.

In the kitchen, time seemed to have stopped somewhere in the 1970s. Harvest gold appliances and worn linoleum flooring told the story of his grandmother's last major renovation. But even here, hidden beneath decades of outdated style choices, lay the potential for something wonderful. The original brick cooking fireplace still anchored one wall, and the butler's pantry's glass-fronted cabinets just needed a good cleaning to restore their charm.

"Okay," he muttered. "New appliances, obviously. Updated electrical. Refinish the cabinets... or maybe all new."

Ryan's footsteps echoed through the empty house. He climbed the stairs to the second floor. Seven spacious bedrooms that would become the heart of his bed-and-breakfast dream. Each room held its own character: corner views of the mountains, tall elegant windows that allowed sunlight to stream in, original fireplace mantels, elegant moldings that spoke to the craftsmanship of a bygone era.

His phone buzzed again, a text from his father: "Did you make it to Laurel Ridge okay? Are you sure about this?"

Ryan quickly replied, "I got here fine, just arrived."

"Good. Have you given any more thought to what I suggested?"

"Yes, Dad. I've thought it over, and my answer hasn't changed. I'm renovating the house. This is home now."

He waited for a response, but none came. With a sigh, Ryan shook his head. His parents just couldn't understand why he felt the need to build a new life in the quiet little town they had left behind so long ago.

He headed outside to tackle the camper setup with the same precision he'd once applied to market analyses. The leveling jacks gave him some trouble—apparently watching YouTube tutorials wasn't quite the same as the actual experience—but eventually, he had his home-away-from-home stabilized behind the farmhouse.

Ryan stood in the doorway of the camper, surveying his new temporary home. It was a stark contrast to his sleek Chicago apartment—but to him; it was a welcome change. The space was modest, yet charming, with just enough room to suit his needs. A compact kitchenette with polished counters and a stove top occupied one corner, ready for simple, satisfying meals. A cozy sitting nook upholstered in earth-toned fabric beckoned him to unwind after a long day's drive.

Beyond that, a sleeping area with soft linens promised restful nights. It wasn't luxurious, but it was comfortable—a place that felt refreshingly unpretentious and uniquely his.

He should unpack and call his mother back. Instead, he found himself walking the overgrown path to the old barn. The door protested but yielded to his push. The smell of aged wood and memories washed over him.

His grandfather's workbench stood exactly as he remembered. A few tools still hanging on the wall, others had been packed away safely in storage totes. A half-finished birdhouse gathered dust in one corner. He ran a hand over the workbench's scarred surface, remembering summer days spent here, learning the difference between various wood grains and how to read a level.

"I could use your advice right about now," he said to the empty space. "Especially with the work that lays ahead for me."

The silence answered with memories: his grandfather's patient voice explaining the importance of proper joint angles, his grandmother bringing them lemonade and cookies, the simple peace of working with his hands. Different from the crushing pressure of corporate boardrooms and ethical compromises.

He thought about that last merger deal in Chicago, the one that had finally pushed him over the edge. The numbers had looked perfect on paper until he'd dug deeper and found the human cost buried in footnotes and fine print. His supervisors had called it "standard business practice." His grandfather would have called it something else entirely.

A sudden gust of wind rattled the barn windows, snapping Ryan back to the present. He had work to do, lists to review, unpacking, and making his temporary home livable. Tomorrow would bring the beginning of actual renovation work. The enormity of it all pressed against his chest, a weight both terrifying and exhilarating.

Back in the camper, Ryan flipped open his laptop. The Wi-Fi hotspot signal struggled, but eventually connected. Between YouTube videos, his grandfather's old notebooks, and sheer determination, he'd figure this out.

His phone buzzed again. A text from his best friend back in Chicago: "How's the voluntary exile going? The suits miss you here in the concrete jungle."

Ryan typed back: "Traded concrete for country living. Life is good."

The response came quickly: "You're crazy, man. But the good kind of crazy. Keep me posted."

Crazy. Maybe. But as Ryan settled into his camper's small dinette to review renovation plans, he felt more sane than he had in years. No hidden agendas, no ethical gray areas—just wood and nails and the chance to build something that mattered... a life on his own terms.

Ryan opened the window beside him, running a hand through his hair. The mountain air, now cooler, carried the first whispers of evening. From the creek that meandered through the back of the property, a choir of spring peepers had begun their nightly symphony. It was a strange paradox—everything felt intimately familiar, yet oddly foreign, like stepping into a dream without understanding its logic.

He thought about his corner office in Chicago, the view of Lake Michigan he'd barely noticed in those final months. The countless meetings where he'd sat silent, watching his colleagues push through deals that skirted ethical lines with practiced ease. He recalled the moment he'd finally stood up and walked away from all of it, his integrity intact but his future uncertain.

"For I know the plans I have for you," he quoted softly, remembering his grandmother's favorite Bible verse. "Plans to prosper you and not to harm you, plans to give you hope and a future."

The words settled something in his spirit, just as they had when she'd spoken them to him as a child. He might not know exactly how to transform or fix everything in the beloved old farmhouse and turn it into the sanctuary he envisioned, but he knew with absolute certainty that this was where he was meant to be.

Tomorrow, he'd begin the work of turning this dream into reality. But for tonight, he let himself simply be present in this moment of new beginnings, surrounded by the whispered memories of the past and the infinite possibilities of the future.

He watched the old porch swing on the back porch of the farmhouse as it creaked gently in the evening breeze, a sound as familiar as his own heartbeat. Somewhere in the distance, a whippoorwill called, its plaintive song echoing across the valley. Ryan closed his eyes and smiled, feeling more at peace than he had in years.

"Welcome home," he whispered to himself, and this time, the words felt absolutely right.

Chapter 3

Faith stepped into the sterile hallway of Mercy Regional Medical Center with the same determination she brought to every job site. Her work boots thudded softly against the gleaming linoleum floor, but today they felt heavier. The buzzing of the fluorescent lights mixed with the faint chatter of hospital staff and monitors, creating a constant background noise she wanted to escape. A nurse passed her, offering a polite smile, but Faith's focus remained ahead. Her appointment with Dr. Benson was at ten sharp, and it was already six minutes past.

She hated being late, but two unexpected phone calls, one from a supplier and one from a potential client with a million questions, had stolen those precious minutes. Sliding her phone into her back pocket, she tugged on the strap of her purse and squared her shoulders as if bracing for another emergency.

The plaque on the door read: Amelia Benson, MD: Cardiology. Faith took a breath, knocked twice, and stepped in before hesitation could take root.

Dr. Benson glanced up from her desk, her kind yet precise demeanor immediately putting Faith on alert. She was in her early forties, wearing a white coat over a crisp blue blouse, with steely gray eyes that didn't miss much. The desk, piled with neat stacks of patient files, radiated the same efficiency Dr. Benson seemed to embody.

"Faith," she greeted with a small smile, standing to shake her hand. "Thank you for coming in."

"Of course," Faith replied, gripping her hand firmly. "Your nurse said it was important."

"And it is." Dr. Benson motioned to the chair across from her desk as she resumed her seat. "How's your father holding up?"

Faith sat, placing her hands in her lap to keep from fidgeting. "He's... determined," she admitted. "He keeps saying things like, 'This hospital food is going to kill me faster than the heart thing.'" She cracked a weak smile, half-hoping for a laugh.

Dr. Benson gave a knowing chuckle. "Sounds about right. Stubbornness has its advantages, but it also means we have to be more cautious with him. His condition requires both physical and mental restraint, neither of which comes easily to men like your father."

Faith's hope for levity quickly faded. "So, what's the latest? Is the medication working?"

Dr. Benson leaned forward slightly, resting her forearms on the desk. Her voice softened, but her tone carried a weight that settled firmly on Faith's chest. "Your father's condition is critical, Faith. His cardiomyopathy—the weakening of his heart muscle—has been progressing for years, likely longer than he's let on."

Faith flinched at the implied secrecy, but stayed quiet.

"Currently, his ejection fraction—the measure of how much blood his heart pumps out with each beat—is down to 35%. For context, a healthy heart operates between 50 and 70%. At 35%, the heart isn't able to supply the body with as much oxygen-rich blood as it needs, especially during exertion."

Faith's brow furrowed. "So… what does that mean day-to-day? Is he in danger right now?"

"Right now, he's stable," Dr. Benson assured her gently. "But his condition is a ticking clock. Without proper management, which includes medication, lifestyle changes, and close monitoring, he's at an increasing risk for complications like heart failure, arrhythmias, or even sudden cardiac arrest."

The words hit Faith like a hammer, breaking through any notion that this could all just go away.

Dr. Benson paused, letting the information settle. "His high blood pressure has exacerbated the condition over time, forcing his heart to work harder than it should. We're addressing that with ACE inhibitors to relax his blood vessels and beta-blockers to reduce the heart's workload and improve its efficiency. But these are not cures. They're management tools."

Faith swallowed hard, her mouth suddenly dry. "And the stress test next week?"

"It'll give us a clearer picture of his heart's capacity under controlled conditions," Dr. Benson explained. "But the bottom line is that he needs to avoid any physical strain. No more heavy lifting, no more long hours. His heart can't handle it."

Faith slumped back slightly in her chair, absorbing the sheer gravity of the situation. "You're saying he can't work?"

Dr. Benson nodded. "Not in the way he's used to. It's imperative that he rest and adhere to the treatment plan if he wants to have any chance at stabilizing. And even then, there's no guarantee his condition won't worsen."

The room fell silent except for the faint ticking of a clock on the wall and hurried footsteps in the hallway. Faith's mind raced, churning through questions and worst-case scenarios.

"What about surgery?" she asked finally. "Or... I don't know, something more aggressive?"

"Surgery isn't off the table in the long term," Dr. Benson said carefully, "but it's not a viable option right now. His heart's too weak to withstand major procedures. If his condition doesn't improve or if he develops life-threatening arrhythmias, we might consider something like an implantable cardioverter-defibrillator—a device that helps regulate abnormal heart rhythms. But that's down the line."

Faith's hands tightened into fists in her lap. "So, this is it? Just... meds and hoping for the best?"

Dr. Benson's voice softened further. "Faith, I know this is hard to hear. But your father's condition isn't something we can fix—it's something we have to manage. And that management is a team effort. You're an important part of that team."

Faith nodded absently, though the truth was she felt like a construction worker handed a blueprint written in a foreign language. She'd spent her life fixing things, taking the broken pieces and putting them back together stronger than before. But this—her father's health—was something she couldn't muscle her way through.

She cleared her throat, forcing herself to focus. "What about..." Her voice faltered for a second before steadying. "What about the stress? I mean, he's worried about the business, about the bills... about me handling everything on my own."

Dr. Benson gave her a sympathetic look. "Stress is one of the worst things for his condition. It's as damaging as physical strain. If he's carrying that kind of worry, it's going to take a toll."

The guilt hit her square in the chest. Of course, he was worried. How could he not be? But wasn't she doing everything she could to keep things afloat?

"What can I do to help?" Faith asked, her voice barely above a whisper.

"Help him feel like he's still part of things," Dr. Benson suggested. "But without letting him overdo it. Involve him in decisions, ask for his advice. Let him see that the legacy he's built is in good hands. And remind him he's not in this alone."

Faith exhaled a trembling breath. Alone. The word struck with a cruel finality, a stark reminder of just how solitary her place in the world had become. Still, this wasn't about her.

"Thank you, Dr. Benson," she said, standing. "I appreciate you walking me through all of this."

"You're doing a lot, Faith," Dr. Benson said kindly. "Don't be afraid to lean on others when you need to."

Faith forced a tight-lipped smile. "I'll keep that in mind."

***

The walk to her father's room felt longer than usual, every step weighted by the conversation she'd just had. When she reached the door to room 412, she paused, her hand hovering over the doorknob. Taking a steadying breath, she pushed it open.

James McNeil lay asleep in the narrow hospital bed, his face pale against the stark white pillow. The steady beep of the heart monitor broke the silence, each note a stark reminder of the delicate rhythm tethering him to life. Tubes and cords snaked in every direction, connecting him to machines that blinked and hummed incessantly. In that moment, it struck her—these lifeless devices were the very things keeping her father alive.

Faith stepped in quietly, careful not to wake him. He looked... smaller somehow, his broad shoulders hunched and his hands resting limply at his sides. These were the same hands that had taught her to hold a hammer, to sand a plank of wood until it was smooth as silk. Seeing them now, bandaged and still, sent a pang through her chest. This once towering figure of a man was fading before her eyes, and it shattered her heart. How could she face a world without her father? The thought was simply unimaginable.

She settled into the chair beside his bed, studying his face. His beard, once full and dark, was now peppered heavily with gray. Lines etched deep into his skin told the story of decades spent outdoors under the sun, working hard to build something lasting.

Her gaze drifted to the bedside table, where an all-too-familiar item caught her eye: a small, worn New Testament, its leather cover scuffed and edges frayed.

She frowned. Her father had always worn his faith openly, giving thanks before every meal and speaking of God with unwavering conviction. Seeing that now stirred a heaviness in her chest. She had turned away from her faith years ago, and she knew that her estrangement from it pained him. Perhaps she should try harder to let go of the past, to rediscover God's word—not for herself, but to bring her father some peace.

Leaning back in the chair, Faith rubbed her temples. Dr. Benson's words played on repeat in her mind: "Let him see the legacy he's built is in good hands." But was it? Could she really handle the weight of his business, his dreams... everything?

She reached out, her fingers brushing the blanket that covered his chest. "You're going to have to stick around, old man," she murmured, her voice cracking slightly. "Because I can't do this without you. I don't care what the doctors say."

Her eyes prickled, but she blinked back the tears. She wasn't the crying type. She never had been.

And yet, as she stood to leave, one thought lingered in her mind: "I can fix a mantelpiece, a deck, even a whole house... but how do you fix a heart?"

Chapter 4

The aroma of sizzling bacon and freshly brewed coffee greeted Ryan as he stepped into Martha's Diner, transporting him instantly back to his childhood. Memories flooded in—all the time's he had been here with his grandparents, savoring hearty breakfasts and engaging in lighthearted conversations with the locals, sharing milkshakes with his buddies on carefree Saturday nights, and nervously fumbling through his first-ever date right here under the fluorescent lights. Everything about the diner was the same, like a time capsule of Laurel Ridge's essence. The chalkboard menu still boasted "Martha's Apple Pie—Best in the County!" in its bold, slightly uneven handwriting, and the place still radiated the same warm, unchanging charm that had always made it feel like home.

Scanning the room, Ryan quickly spotted Mark Winslow lounging in a corner booth, one arm slung casually across the backrest, his other hand scrolling lazily on his phone. Mark still carried the easy confidence Ryan remembered from childhood, now paired with the polished look of his banker suit and tie. Yet beneath the refined exterior, Ryan could still see the teenage boy who had once cannon balled off the Dalton farmhouse creek rope swing with wild abandon.

Mark looked up just as Ryan sauntered over, his trademark half-grin appearing the moment their eyes met. "Well, I'll be," Mark said, setting his phone down and standing to slap Ryan on the back. "Ryan Dalton, in the flesh! I half-expected you to send some city slicker assistant to meet me instead."

Ryan chuckled and extended a hand, which Mark immediately brushed aside in favor of a quick brotherly hug. "Assistant? Those days are far behind, buddy. You're looking at a one-man show now."

"Right," Mark drawled, as they both slid into the booth. "The big time city boy comes back home to his roots. I can't wait to see how this unfolds."

Ryan arched a brow and leaned back in the booth. "Says the guy who went from mowing lawns to giving investment advice. How are the stock markets treating you, huh? All solid predictions and no regret?"

"I'm a banker, not a mind reader," Mark fired back, waving a hand dismissively. "Enough about me. You're the one everyone's buzzing about. I can't head anywhere in this town without hearing, 'Did you hear Ryan Dalton's back? Gonna fix up Eleanor and Frank's property and make it a bed-and-breakfast.' So, spill. How's it feel being the town celebrity?"

Ryan snorted, shaking his head. "Celebrity? All I've done is step on more nails in 24 hours than I care to count, and I've discovered rodents really love century-old insulation."

"Well," Mark said thoughtfully, picking up his coffee cup, "sounds like you're living the dream—if the dream involves tetanus shots and evicting squatters, that is."

Before Ryan could retort, a booming, cheerful voice interrupted their banter. "Ryan Thomas Dalton, is that you?"

Both men turned to see Martha Kincaid striding toward them, her floral apron swinging and her coffee pot firmly in hand. Her rounded face glowed with warmth and excitement, her blue eyes twinkling as she openly studied Ryan like he'd risen from folklore.

"Knew it was you the second I laid eyes on that Dalton jawline," she declared, planting herself in front of the booth with one hand on her hip. "Well, aren't you as tall as the maple tree out back! Last time I saw you, you were about to head to college, strutting around here acting like you owned the place. And now here you are again, all grown up. Mercy, don't you have the look of your granddaddy about you!"

Ryan couldn't stop the grin that tugged at his lips. "Good to see you too, Martha," he said, rising slightly out of respect as she reached over and gave his arm a hearty pat and then quickly wrapped him in a bear hug.

Martha tilted her head, hands on her hips now. "Good to see me? Boy, please. I'm the one who should be saying that to you. Walking into my diner after all these years. Nearly gave me a heart attack."

She didn't wait for an invitation before grabbing a chair from a table nearby and plopping down, setting the coffeepot on the table as though making it known she was staying. "Now then, tell me more about what's brought you back home, Ryan? Don't tell me you missed my pancakes that badly."

"It's a long story," Ryan began, but she quickly waved off any hesitation.

"Lord knows I've got all the time in the world to sit and hear it," Martha said with a wink. "So, out with it, Ryan. Don't leave me in suspense."

Ryan chuckled, leaning back slightly. "I've traded boardrooms and skyscrapers for country air, Martha. I'm renovating my grandparents' farmhouse and turning it into a bed-and-breakfast."

Martha tilted her head, her sharp blue eyes narrowing, though her expression softened with a touch of admiration. "Well, would you look at that? A big-city man rolling up his sleeves and coming back to build something that matters. I've got to say, I'm impressed."

Mark leaned forward with a sly grin. "You should be, Martha. If anyone can turn a dream into reality, it's him."

Martha's face grew thoughtful for a moment, and then she smiled warmly. "I bet your grandparents are smiling in heaven right now, proud as can be, watching their boy. You're making them proud, Ryan."

Ryan smiled and sipped the coffee Martha had poured him without asking. It was strong and bitter—just the way he remembered it.

"So," Martha said, her tone softening slightly. "Your mama and daddy. They doing okay? How're they taking it? You moving back here, I mean? I always thought your daddy especially wanted to keep you out there in the big leagues."

Ryan hesitated, cupping his coffee mug loosely to give himself a moment. "They... mean well, Martha. They really do. But I'm not sure they understand why I'm doing this. Mom keeps telling me the university has a position if I want it—prestigious, tenured, the works. And Dad, well... you know him. He's more 'let's plan everything down to the last decimal point.' So, from where they're sitting, this move must look like I'm throwing everything away."

"Listen, Ryan," Martha said, patting his arm. "Sometimes parents have their dreams for their child so packed full of love they forget to leave enough room for your own. But if you're honoring what God's put on your heart—and goodness knows it sounds like you are—then don't you go worrying about disappointing them. They'll find their way to seeing it someday. And if they don't, well, love forgives even stubbornness."

"That's the plan," Ryan said softly, rubbing the back of his neck. "Keep moving forward. Build the kind of life I want."

"Oh, you'll do more than that. I have faith," Martha replied with conviction, leaning back in her chair. "And when you get to where you're going, you'll see—you'll look back and know every bit of it was worth it."

She rose then, smoothing her apron and grabbing the coffee pot. "Now you boys behave," she said, wagging a playful finger. "And Ryan? I've missed you."

And as Ryan watched her retreat toward the counter, her broad frame silhouetted in the morning activity of the diner, he felt it—a swelling sense of hope that perhaps, against the backdrop of mountain air and old friendships, he really could make this vision a reality.

"She's something else," Mark said, laughing softly as he raised his coffee cup.

"That she is," Ryan replied with a grin.

"So, what's on your agenda today?" Mark asked.

Ryan took a sip of his coffee, setting the mug down with a soft clink. "I'm heading over to McNeil Construction after this. I'm hoping to hire them for some of the work on the farmhouse. You know the place? What's your take on them?"

Mark leaned back, folding his arms with a thoughtful expression. "McNeil Construction, huh? Well, if you want the best in town, you're looking in the right direction. James McNeil built many of the houses in this county, including my parents' home, so the man knows his stuff. Of course, with his health issues, his daughter Faith's the one running the show now."

Ryan raised a curious brow. "Faith?"

"Faith McNeil," Mark said with a knowing grin. "She's been a part of McNeil Construction before she even graduated from high school. Tough as nails, sharp as a saw blade, and probably the most skilled carpenter I've ever seen. She's got James's knack for the craft and a head for business that makes her a force to reckon with. But fair warning—she doesn't suffer fools lightly."

Ryan smirked, intrigued. "So, what are you saying? That she'll give me a hard time?"

Mark chuckled. "Let's just say Faith is in a league of her own. She's the only female contractor around here, and honestly? She's better than most of the men in the business."

Ryan leaned back in his seat, considering. "Well, there are plenty of women in the world who can outperform some men. Is she level-headed, easy to work with?"

Mark shrugged, finishing the last of his coffee. "Easy to work with? I'd say yes, after you get to know her. Deep down, Faith's one of the most loyal people you'll ever meet. She just hasn't had it easy, you know? She's had to work twice as hard as anyone else to prove herself, and not everyone around here is ready to give credit where it's due."

Ryan nodded, storing away the insights. If Faith McNeil was as talented as Mark made her out to be, then landing her for the renovation could be a game-changer. And if she was as tough as he described, well, Ryan had never backed down from a challenge.

Mark stood, sliding out of the booth and tossing a few bills on the table. "Anyway, I've got to get going—big meeting at the bank this morning," Mark said, sliding out of the booth and grabbing his blazer. "But as for McNeil Construction? Solid crew. They've got a great reputation around here, and they know their stuff. Definitely worth your time to swing by and talk to them—you won't regret it."

Ryan nodded as he stood to follow Mark out of the diner. "Thanks for the advice."

Mark grinned, clapping Ryan on the back as they headed toward the door. "Well, you know where to find me if you need anything. Swing by the bank anytime, and count on seeing me soon, buddy. I'll lend a hand wherever I can while you're renovating. Don't let the suit fool you. I still know my way around a hammer and nails."

Chapter 5

Monica's voice carried through the open office door. "Faith, you've got a visitor."

Faith glanced up from the stack of medical bills she'd been trying to decode, quickly sliding them under a folder. She wasn't in the mood for visitors, not with her father's latest test results weighing on her mind and the Rogers' mantelpiece deadline looming.

"This is Ryan Dalton," Monica continued, ushering in a tall man with the kind of easy smile Faith usually associated with salespeople and politicians. "He's looking to discuss a renovation project."

Ryan stepped forward, extending his hand. "Nice to meet you, Ms. McNeil."

Faith rose, noting his firm handshake and the fresh scuffs on what were clearly brand-new work boots. Another weekend warrior with more enthusiasm than experience, probably. Just what she needed. Ryan Dalton had a polished, city-slicker vibe about him—a clean-shaven face, wavy hair so impeccably styled it could have been cut from a glossy magazine page, and jeans that still carried the crispness of a recent purchase. Yet, it was his eyes that drew you in, twinkling with a magnetic charm that hinted at something deeper beneath his polished exterior.

"Mark Winslow called early and mentioned you might be coming by," she said, gesturing to the chair across from her desk. "How is our friendly neighborhood banker?"

"Still trying to convince everyone he was the star quarterback in high school," Ryan replied, settling into the chair. "Though I distinctly remember him spending more time on the bench than on the field."

The comment surprised a laugh out of Faith. "You went to school together?"

"Born and raised here, actually. Just moved back after a decade in Chicago." Ryan's hazel eyes swept the office, taking in the framed blueprints and project photos. "The Dalton farmhouse on Ridge Road? That's the project that called me back home."

Faith's interest sharpened. She knew that property—everyone in Laurel Ridge did. The sprawling old house had been empty for years, its slow decay a frequent topic of conversation among locals who remembered its former glory.

"Your project?" she asked, careful to keep her tone neutral. "What exactly are you planning?"

"A bed-and-breakfast." Ryan's enthusiasm was apparent in the way he leaned forward, hands gesturing as he spoke. "My grandparents left me the property, and I want to restore it, make it something special again. I'm handling some of the work myself—the master bedroom, library, and kitchen—but I need help with the rest. The wrap-around porch alone is going to be a challenge."

Faith's eyebrows rose. "You're going to do some of the renovation work yourself?"

"Yep." He had the grace to look slightly sheepish. "I learned the basics from my grandfather when I was younger. He owned Dalton Construction a long time ago."

"Frank Dalton was your grandfather?" That explained a few things. Old Frank Dalton had been a legend in local construction circles before retiring.

"He taught me enough to be dangerous," Ryan admitted. "Though I'll admit, my skills are a bit rusty after years behind a desk. That's why I'm here."

Faith studied him, noting the contrast between his confident tone and the uncertainty that flickered in his eyes when he mentioned his construction skills. "What exactly did you do in Chicago?"

"Financial analyst. Mergers and acquisitions." He said it like he was confessing to a questionable past. "But I'm ready for a change. I need something different in my life. Something real."

"Real enough to require permits, inspections, and probably a lot of money," Faith pointed out. "Restoring an old farmhouse isn't the same as watching DIY videos, Mr. Dalton."

"Trust me, I'm well aware of my limitations." Ryan's smile turned self-deprecating. "I spent yesterday trying to level a camper trailer. Let's just say YouTube tutorials have their shortcomings."

Faith tried not to smile at the mental image. "You're living in a camper?"

"Behind the house. It's temporary." He shrugged. "Seemed more practical than commuting from a hotel while work's being done on the house."

"So, let me get this straight," she said, her brow knitted in concentration as she attempted to unravel the puzzle. "You had an entire life in Chicago—you lived there, worked there. And now you're back here, planning to live in a camper while renovating a farmhouse that's been abandoned for years?"

"That's the gist of it," he confirmed with a grin.

"But... why?"

His smile widened, sending a faint but unmistakable warmth creeping up her neck. "I know—it sounds crazy. My parents think so too. But life has a funny way of steering us where we need to go. I was ready for a change. So, I sold my condo, sold nearly everything I owned, bought a camper, and hit the road. And here I am."

Something about his practical thinking softened Faith's skepticism slightly.

"Listen," Ryan continued, "I get it—this probably sounds a little out there. You're most likely wondering, 'Is this guy serious?' But trust me, I've thought this through. I understand the farmhouse is a big project, and I promise I haven't lost my mind. From what I've heard, McNeil Construction is the best around for this kind of work. Mark mentioned you specialize in renovations, and that's exactly why I'm here—I want to hire your team."

"We do specialize in renovations, among other things." Faith reached for her tablet, pulling up their current project schedule. The Rogers' job would be wrapping up soon, and the Madison project wasn't set to begin for a month. She had a huge crew to do the job. And bottom line, she welcomed the potential income. The timing of this project could work, assuming the farmhouse didn't spiral into a long-drawn-out money pit project. "Have you had the property assessed? Gotten any permits? Blueprints? Anything?"

Ryan handed over a folder. "Most of what I have so far is in there, along with some preliminary plans I drew up. The blueprints are back in the camper."

Faith took the folder and thumbed through its contents. The preliminary plans varied from meticulously detailed bullet-point lists to hand-drawn sketches adorned with sticky notes capturing his thoughts on various rooms in the house. She couldn't help but grin at the sticky notes, amused by the occasional humorous comments he'd jotted down.

"Sorry to interrupt, but Tom needs your approval on the lumber order for the Madison project. He's leaving for the supplier in twenty minutes," Monica said with a knock on the door.

Faith nodded. "I'll be right there." She turned back to Ryan. "I need to handle this, but I'd like to see the property firsthand before we discuss anything further. Are you free this afternoon?"

"Absolutely." Ryan's face lit up with undisguised enthusiasm. "Any time that works for you."

"One o'clock?" At his nod, Faith stood. "Good. We'll do a walk-through, see exactly what we're dealing with."

"Perfect." Ryan rose, gathering his papers. "And thank you, Ms. McNeil. I know this is a big project—"

"Faith," she corrected automatically. "And don't thank me yet. I haven't agreed to anything."

His smile widened. "Fair enough. But I have a good feeling about this."

Faith watched him follow Monica out, noting the way he stopped to admire the hand-carved trim around her office door—genuine interest, not just polite observation. Maybe he had learned something from his grandfather after all.

"Well?" Monica reappeared a moment later, eyebrows raised expectantly.

"Well, what?"

"Don't play dumb with me, Faith McNeil. I can tell you're interested in this project. And that man was pretty easy on the eyes, too."

"Interested... yes," Faith said, gathering the papers for Tom's lumber order.

Monica's knowing smile was irritating.

"Don't start." Faith brushed past her friend, heading for Tom's office.

Monica fell into step beside her. "Admit it—you're intrigued. The Dalton farmhouse is a piece of local history. And the man planning to renovate the home..."

"Monica." Faith's tone carried a warning.

"Fine, fine." Monica held up her hands in surrender. "I'm just saying, sometimes God puts opportunities in our path for a reason."

Faith shot her friend a look. "Really? You're playing the God card?"

"If the scripture fits..." Monica's grin was unrepentant. "One o'clock, huh? That gives you just enough time to finish the Rogers' paperwork and change into a shirt that isn't covered in sawdust."

Faith glanced down at her work clothes, noting the wood shavings clinging to her flannel shirt. "I'm not changing. This is a work meeting, not a date."

"Of course it is." Monica's tone was far too innocent. "But maybe brush the sawdust out of your hair? Just a suggestion."

Faith ignored her, ducking into Tom's office before Monica could offer any more helpful advice. She had more important things to worry about than impressing Ryan Dalton. Like how she was going to keep the company afloat if her father's medical condition didn't improve soon.

Still, as she reviewed lumber specifications with Tom, her mind kept drifting to the Dalton farmhouse. She'd driven past it countless times, watching its slow decline and thinking what a shame it was to see such craftsmanship go to waste. The prospect of restoring it was admittedly tempting, both professionally and financially.

But something about Ryan Dalton made her uneasy. Not in a bad way, exactly. More like the feeling you got standing too close to a live wire—that awareness of potential energy, of something that could either power your whole house or shock you senseless if you weren't careful.

Faith had learned early in life that it was safer to stick to what you could measure and control. Wood. Numbers. Concrete plans. Ryan Dalton, with his easy smile and ambitious dreams, didn't fit into any of those categories.

Chapter 6

The front steps creaked under Faith's boots as she followed Ryan onto the wraparound porch of the farmhouse. She automatically cataloged each sound: the hollow protest of rotting wood, the subtle give of weakened joists, the whisper of loose nails working free.

"I know," Ryan said, catching her expression. "The porch is first on the priority list."

"The porch shouldn't be anyone's priority until we verify the foundation's condition." Faith crouched down, peering between the weathered floorboards. "When did you say the last structural inspection was?"

"A few weeks ago." Ryan produced a folded paper from his back pocket. "Pete Harrison did the honors. Said the foundation's solid, just needs some repointing in spots."

Faith straightened, surprised. "Really?"

Ryan nodded. "Mark recommended him. Said he's the best."

Points for not dawdling, Faith admitted silently. She accepted the paper, scanning Pete's detailed notes. The foundation was indeed sound. The limestone blocks were still true after more than a century, with only minor deterioration in the mortar. At least Ryan wouldn't be building his dreams on shifting sand.

"Show me the rest," she said, tucking the paper under her arm.

Ryan's face lit up as he led her to the front door. The door resisted slightly, and Faith observed how his hands skillfully twisted and lifted the doorknob in unison.

Inside, dust motes swirled in shafts of afternoon light. Faith's trained eye took in the essentials: original hardwood floors under years of grime, intact crown molding, plaster walls showing typical age cracks but no serious damage. Peeling wallpaper. The foyer's grand staircase curved upward, its mahogany banister dulled but unwarped.

"Main floor first?" Ryan suggested. "I'm planning to handle the master bedroom and bath, the library and kitchen myself, but I'll entertain your professional opinion."

Faith nodded, following him through a set of pocket doors into what had obviously been a formal parlor. The room's proportions were classic Victorian, with tall windows and a marble fireplace that would have been the height of luxury when the house was built.

"This'll be the main gathering space for guests," Ryan explained, his enthusiasm evident in the way he gestured. "Morning coffee, afternoon tea, that sort of thing. The original fireplace just needs cleaning and—why are you smiling?"

Faith quickly schooled her expression. "Nothing. Just... your boots."

Ryan glanced down at his pristine work boots, then at Faith's well-worn ones. "My boots?"

"Let's just say they've clearly never seen a day of work... yet. Do you understand what you're getting into?" The words came out gentler than she'd intended, softened by the earnest way he was trying.

He ran a hand through his dark hair; the gesture making it stand up slightly. Faith determinedly ignored how the afternoon light caught the waves he'd created. "You cut right to the chase, don't you. Look, I know I must seem like a joke to someone with your experience."

"Not a joke," Faith corrected, moving to examine the fireplace's tile work. "Just... optimistic... hopeful... Maybe getting himself in too deep."

"Is that a polite way of saying naïve?"

"That too." She turned back to find him watching her, his hazel eyes warm with amusement rather than offense. Something fluttered in her chest, and she quickly looked away. "The kitchen... let me take a look at it."

Ryan led her through a butler's pantry that would need complete restoration. The kitchen beyond was a study in decades of questionable choices: 1970s cabinets, peeling linoleum, and appliances that belonged in a museum.

"This is where I'll start," Ryan said, spreading his hands to encompass the space. "Strip it down to the bones, rebuild from scratch. I want this room more modern and functional, but keep some of the older details. And that... I'm keeping that."

He pointed to a massive brick cooking fireplace, its arch still perfectly true after more than a century. Faith stepped closer, admiring the craftsmanship. The bricks had been laid with the kind of care you rarely saw anymore, each one placed just so.

"Smart choice," she said. "This is a piece of history."

"My grandmother used to tell stories about learning to bake bread in that oven." Ryan's voice softened with memory. "Said you could tell the day's weather by how the fire drew."

Faith glanced at him, caught off guard by the way nostalgia transformed his features. For a moment, she could see past the polished city boy exterior to something more genuine—a man trying to preserve more than just a building.

The moment broke when a floorboard creaked under her foot. Faith cleared her throat. "The library?"

Ryan's enthusiasm returned as he led her to the next room. "My grandparents loved this room. Built-in bookcases, original fireplace... though I've got some water damage in that corner."

Faith examined the stained ceiling and walls, mentally calculating the extent of the repair needed. The bookcases were indeed beautiful, their craftsmanship evident even under years of neglect. "These are quarter-sawn oak. Don't try to strip them too fast—one wrong move with a heat gun, and you'll ruin them."

"Noted." Ryan made a face. "Though I'm starting to think my DIY list might need some adjusting."

"You think?" The words came out drier than she'd intended, but Ryan just laughed.

"Come on," he said, heading for the stairs. "Wait till you see what I'm dealing with upstairs. Or should I say, you and your crew may be dealing with"

Faith followed, noting how the staircase was solid under their combined weight.

She tried not to notice how Ryan's shoulders filled out his work shirt, or the way his too-new jeans actually fit rather well. This was a business assessment, nothing more.

The second floor was a warren of bedrooms and baths, all needing varying degrees of renovation. Ryan walked her through each space, outlining his vision for guest rooms with en suite bathrooms and period-appropriate fixtures.

"I'm thinking seven rooms total," he explained, leading her into what had obviously been the master suite. "This is another room that I intend to renovate myself."

Faith took in the assortment of tools on the floor, the folding table covered in renovation books, the single lamp casting odd shadows in the corners. "Cozy."

"Hey, it has potential. I figured I could handle renovating this room." Ryan gestured to the bay window overlooking the overgrown gardens. "And the view's not bad."

Faith had to agree. The late afternoon light painted the mountains in shades of blue and purple, layer upon layer fading into the distance. Even through grimy windows, it was breathtaking.

"My grandmother used to sit here for hours," Ryan said quietly. "Said she could watch the whole world change color."

Something in his tone made Faith turn. He was staring out the window, his profile etched against the light, and for a moment she saw him clearly—not as the overconfident former financier, but as someone seeking something real in a world that often felt anything but.

She knew that feeling. Knew it in the way her hands sought out wood grain when her mind was troubled, in the satisfaction of building something solid in a world full of uncertainty. In the weight of legacy and expectation, and the fear of letting it all slip away.

She moved closer to one of the nearby windows, her gaze sweeping over the property behind the house. Her eyes landed on the camper parked conspicuously in the overgrown yard, its sleek, modern appearance clashing with the rustic charm of its surroundings.

"Well," she said, tilting her head toward the camper, "is that your long-term plan? To stay in the camper? Or do you see yourself actually living in the house once it's up and running as a bed-and-breakfast?"

Ryan turned to her, a small smile tugging at the corner of his lips. "The camper's just a temporary solution. Figured it made more sense to invest in something like that rather than pouring money into a rental. Once the bed-and-breakfast is up and running, I'll move into this room while I work on building a house of my own further back on the property. There's a spot out there I've already picked—it's perfect. When I'm done, I'll either sell the camper or keep it for future travels if time ever allows."

She raised a brow, clearly impressed. "Sounds like you've thought it all out."

"Trying to," he said, his tone steady but humble.

Faith turned back to her clipboard. "I noticed when I pulled in, the roof probably needs a complete replacement. And these windows—they're original, but they'll leak heat like sieves unless they're properly restored."

"I know it's a lot." Ryan's voice was quiet but determined. "But I also know it's worth doing right. That's why I need McNeil Construction. Your reputation for historical renovation is exactly what this place deserves."

Faith studied him, weighing his words against her instincts. "Why this? Why now? I assume you had a successful career in Chicago."

Ryan was quiet for a moment, considering. "You ever look at your life and realize you're building something that looks perfect on paper, but feels hollow inside?"

The question hit closer to home than Faith wanted to admit. She thought of her father's hospital bills, of the Madison project's tight margins, of all the careful plans for her future that now felt increasingly fragile.

"Look," Ryan continued, "I know I'm not the typical client. I'm learning as I go and want to do some of the work myself, and I'll probably make tons of mistakes. But it's important to me. This place? It matters. Not just as a business venture, but as a piece of history. Of family. I want to do it right."

Faith moved to the window again, buying time to think. The garden below was a tangle of overgrown shrubs and volunteer saplings, but she could see the bones of what it had been—what it could be again. Like the house itself, it just needed someone willing to put in the work.

"If we do this," she said finally, "you follow our lead on the structural work. No YouTube tutorials, no weekend warrior experiments. Not on the load-bearing elements."

Hope flickered across Ryan's face. "Does that mean you're considering it?"

"I'm considering it." Faith turned back to her clipboard, all business again. "I'll need to review Pete's full report, draw up detailed estimates. The porch alone will be a major undertaking."

"But it's possible?"

Faith met his eyes, finding them filled with an earnestness that made her chest tight. "It's possible. Not easy, not cheap, but possible."

Ryan's smile was like watching a sunrise break over the mountains—steady, inevitable, warming everything it touched. Faith quickly looked away, reminding herself that charm and good intentions wouldn't pay bills or guarantee success.

"I should go," she said, gathering her notes. "I'll have some preliminary numbers for you soon. I'll get right to work on it."

"Thank you." Ryan said as he followed her downstairs. "Really, Faith. I know this isn't a simple project."

"Simple is overrated." Faith paused at the front door, struck by a memory. "My dad always said the best projects are the ones that scare you a little. Keeps you honest."

"Smart man."

"Yeah." Faith swallowed against the sudden tightness in her throat. "He is."

The afternoon sunlight spilled over the tangled expanse of the lawn, casting long shadows. Faith's truck stood waiting, a tangible promise of escape—of returning to the predictable world of schedules and calculations, a realm where everything aligned neatly. She craved that sense of structure now because Ryan was unsettling her balance, introducing a tilt to her world that left her feeling undeniably off-kilter.

"I'll be in touch," she said, forcing herself to sound professionally detached.

Ryan nodded, leaning against one of the porch posts. "I'll be here. Probably watching more YouTube tutorials."

Faith couldn't quite suppress her smile. "Try not to destroy anything historic before I get back to you."

His laughter lingered in the air as she climbed into the truck, rich and unguarded. Faith kept her gaze firmly fixed on the road as she drove off, resisting the urge to glance in the rearview mirror. Her life was already tangled enough without inviting Ryan Dalton's disarming optimism and unexpected complexity into the fray. But oh, that smile—and those eyes...

"Focus, Faith. It's a job—and quite an intriguing one, at that," she said.

As she turned onto the main road, Faith found herself already making mental notes about materials and crew assignments. The Dalton farmhouse would be a challenge, no doubt about that. The question was whether the biggest risk lay in taking on the project—or in working so closely with a man who saw beneath surfaces as easily as she did.

Faith pushed the thought away, focusing on the road ahead. She had estimates to calculate, crews to coordinate, and her father's health and medical bills to worry about. Romance, even the hypothetical kind, had no place in that equation.

No matter how well Ryan Dalton filled out a work shirt.

Chapter 7

Faith stared at the preliminary estimates scattered haphazardly across her desk, each scribbled on whatever scrap of paper had been the closest at hand. A vanilla candle—a small concession to femininity in her otherwise practical space—flickered on the corner of her desk.

The numbers for the Dalton house renovation looked solid. More than solid, actually. Promising for sure. The kind of project that could help ease the strain of her father's medical bills. It should have been an easy decision, a welcome win. And yet, a faint unease tugged at her resolve.

Her mind circled back to Ryan. His genuine enthusiasm, almost disarming in its sincerity, lingered in her thoughts, unsettling in its contrast to the hardened negotiations she was used to. Faith prided herself on her sharp instincts and unwavering confidence, but for reasons she couldn't quite articulate, that assuredness wavered now. Something about this job, about him, made her pause.

"This is ridiculous," she muttered, reaching for her coffee. "It's just another job."

But even as she said it, she knew that wasn't quite true. Most clients didn't look at hundred-year-old houses with a mixture of reverence, excitement, and determination. And they surely didn't dream of turning a farmhouse into a bed-and-breakfast. Most clients didn't insist on living on site in a camper, of all things. And most clients definitely didn't make her wonder what they'd look like with sawdust in their carefully styled hair.

A quick knock on her door interrupted her thoughts. Monica stood there, a smile on her face.

"What?" Faith asked.

"Tell me about the Dalton house." Monica's dark eyes sparkled with amusement. "I've heard so many stories about that place from my parents. Actually, I caught some gossip at the diner this morning about the owner. What's he like?"

"Optimistic to the point of delusion. A definite DIY'er wanna be." Faith tapped her pencil against the estimate sheets. "He wants to actually do some renovations himself. He plans to live in a camper throughout the entire renovation. He has absolutely no idea what lies ahead."

Monica's laugh echoed through the office. "Oh, this is going to be good. Please tell me you took plenty of pictures of the house for the company website."

"There's nothing to take pictures of yet," Faith said. "I haven't decided if we're taking the job."

"Right." Monica leaned forward, her expression turning more serious. "Because restoring a historical house doesn't intrigue you, does it? And having Mr. Ryan Dalton working nearby doesn't add a fun twist to the project, now, does it?"

"I hadn't thought about it."

"Mm hmm." Monica stood, smoothing her skirt. "Well, when you're ready to admit that this project might be something you need or want right now, I'll be at my desk drafting up the proposal and contract. You know where to find me."

Faith watched her friend leave, irritation and affection warring in her chest. Monica had been her best friend since high school, the sister she'd never had, and occasionally Faith wondered if that gave her too much insight into Faith's careful defenses.

Her cell phone rang, the screen lighting up with "Mercy Regional Medical Center." Faith's heart jumped as she grabbed it.

"Daddy? Is everything okay?"

"Can't a father call his daughter without something being wrong?" Faith could hear the fatigue in her father's voice. "Heard some interesting news from Mark Winslow when he stopped by earlier."

"The Dalton place," Faith said, sinking back into her chair. "You know it?"

"Know it? Frank and Eleanor Dalton were quite a force in this town." James said. "Frank was a wealth of information. He shared a lot of tricks of the trade with me. Eleanor used to bring the best peach cobbler you've ever tasted to job sites whenever we were working near her property. I've been in that house many times over the years before they passed. That house has good bones, Faith."

"That's what Mr. Dalton said, and I agree," Faith said,

"Ryan... you know I remember that boy. Strong, smart fella. Him and Mark used to run all over town together back in the day." James chuckled, then coughed slightly. "What do you think of him?"

"He's..." Faith chose her words carefully. "Enthusiastic. Inexperienced. Living in a camper behind the house, if you can believe it. Wants to tackle some of the renovations himself. Seems eager."

"Sounds familiar," James said. "Kind of like someone I know who couldn't wait for her own apartment to be move-in ready. I recall you camping out in the middle of that entire mess with a tent and a sleeping bag while fixing the place up."

"That was different, dad," Faith protested. "I knew what I was doing."

"Everyone has to start somewhere. If he's eager to learn and willing to put in the effort, let him." A moment of silence filled the line. "You know, if I wasn't stuck in this hospital bed..."

"I know, Daddy." Faith swallowed against the sudden tightness in her throat. "How are you feeling today?"

"Better. Dr. Benson says my numbers are improving." Another pause. "Faith, honey, you need to quit worrying about me. Worry about the business. You need this project right now. It'll keep your mind busy and off your ole man."

"The business needs you to get better. I need you to get better."

"I know, but listen honey, maybe..." James's voice softened. "Maybe this project is exactly what you need right now. It sounds like a great challenge to keep your mind busy and give you a break from worrying about me. Sometimes the Lord places opportunities in our path in ways we don't expect."

"Through a city boy who's come back to country living with more dreams than sense?"

"Through people willing to see the potential in things others might write off." Faith could picture her father's knowing smile. "That young man chose to come back home, to honor his grandparent's legacy. Says something about his character, don't you think?"

Faith glanced at the estimate sheets spread across her desk. "Would you take the job? If you could?"

"In a heartbeat." James's voice strengthened. "But I trust your judgment, Faith. You've never steered this company wrong. Just... don't let fear of what might go wrong keep you from seeing what might go right."

"When did you get so wise?"

"About the time you started being so stubborn," he said. "You're just like your old man."

After saying goodbye to her father, Faith pulled up her email account and began to type.

Monica reappeared in the doorway, a knowing smile on her face. "Should I finish the proposal and contract?"

"You were outside my door listening, weren't you?"

"Of course!"

"Yes, go ahead. But make sure the contract is airtight. If he's going to insist on doing some of the renovations himself, we need clear boundaries about what he can and can't do."

"Boundaries." Monica's eyes danced with amusement.

"Yes. Boundaries." Faith straightened in her chair, adopting her most professional tone. "Make it clear, I'm not running a construction tutorial service. What I say goes, and if I tell him it's too dangerous for him to work while the crew and I are on site, then my word is law."

"Wouldn't dream of suggesting otherwise, though it is tempting."

"Out!" Faith pointed to the door, fighting back a laugh as Monica retreated, giggling.

Faith leaned back in her chair, releasing a long, steady breath. The familiar symphony of the workshop hummed outside her door—the whir of the table saw, the measured rhythm of hammers, and the sporadic bursts of laughter from her crew. This was her sanctuary: orderly, predictable, exactly as it should be. The last thing she needed was some charming city boy waltzing in with grand ideas to disrupt her peace. Dreamers, in her experience, were nothing but trouble.

But as she turned to look out her window at the mountains painted in late afternoon light, she couldn't help but remember the way Ryan had looked at his grandparent's house—not seeing the peeling paint and outdated fixtures, but the potential beneath. It was the same way she looked at old homes.

"Just business," she reminded herself firmly, turning back to her computer to finish drafting an email to Ryan. Her fingers hovered over the keyboard as she searched for the right words.

Mr. Dalton,

She backspaced. Too formal.

Ryan,
After careful consideration, McNeil Construction is prepared to take on your renovation project. I'll have a formal proposal and contract ready for your review within forty-eight hours. Please note that while we appreciate your enthusiasm, any hands-on participation will need to be strictly regulated for safety and insurance purposes. Everything will be detailed in the contract that I will provide for your consideration.
If you have any questions, feel free to reach out to me.

Faith McNeil
Project Manager McNeil Construction

She hit send before she could second-guess herself, then sat back, feeling as though she'd just stepped off the edge of something much bigger than a simple renovation project.

"Well," she said. "Here's hoping I just made the right call."

Chapter 8

Ryan knelt in a corner of the kitchen, his tape measure stretched taut. He squinted at the faint pencil marks he'd drawn to outline what would, hopefully, one day become a functional and attractive built in storage area. Jotting down the latest measurement in his notebook, he blew out a breath.

He tugged the tape measure back with a satisfying snap, then stood and surveyed the room. The kitchen, stripped of all the old appliances, was an echo of the kitchen he'd known as a child, where his grandmother hummed hymns while kneading bread and his grandfather poured coffee with slow deliberation. It was slowly transforming, one step at a time. He could imagine the room stripped of the cabinets and countertops that needed updating. Raw. Untamed. A canvas with endless potential.

The low rumble of tires crunching over gravel tugged him out of his thoughts. Ryan furrowed his brow, clipped the tape measure in his back pocket, and grabbed the rag on the counter to wipe the dust from his hands. As he walked to the front of the house, he caught sight of a silver sedan parking.

Mark stepped out of the car with the kind of effortless ease only he could pull off, making his suit look less like formal wear and more like an afterthought. His tie hung loosely around his neck, and his grin—equal parts mischief and familiarity—spread wide as he shrugged off his jacket. With a flick of his wrist, he tossed it into the car, then nudged the door shut with his hip, exuding the relaxed confidence of someone perfectly at ease in his own skin.

Ryan smirked as he opened the front door. "Well, well," he said as Mark trotted up the steps. "I thought bankers didn't make house calls."

Mark glanced at Ryan's flannel shirt and jeans covered in dust and sweat, then did an exaggerated tilt of his head to study the peeling paint above the doorway. "Figured you might need some advice or a shoulder to cry on. Should I start passing out donation cans that say 'Save Ryan Dalton's sanity'?"

Ryan snorted. "Come on in."

Mark stepped inside and let out a low whistle as his gaze flicked around the entryway. "Man. I forgot how huge this place is."

"Yeah," Ryan said with a smile, shoving his hands into his pockets. "It feels different now. Bigger, somehow. Probably because I'm the one responsible for keeping it standing."

Mark slapped him lightly on the shoulder. "Well, it beats spreadsheets and conference calls, right?"

"Sometimes, yes. And sometimes..." Ryan hesitated, looking toward the staircase, where sunlight filtered through the dusty windows at the landing. "Sometimes, I start wondering what I got myself into and if this was a good idea or not."

"Well, I'm voting for a good idea. But," Mark added, raising a finger, "show me what you're working on so I can decide just how much trouble you're in."

Ryan chuckled and gestured for Mark to follow him. "Kitchen. I'm taking measurements and trying to figure out the workflow. No promise you'll be impressed."

Mark trailed after him, his hands stuffed into his dress slacks as he stepped carefully over debris and stacks of supplies. "I'm already impressed. Mostly because you still have all your fingers."

The kitchen was a mosaic of past dreams and future ambitions, a space caught in limbo between nostalgia and necessity. Cabinets, some clinging precariously to their hinges, stood like weary sentinels of another time. The countertops, chipped and scarred with age, bore the weight of decades gone by, while the tired linoleum flooring peeled up at the corners like a neglected page of history. Pencil marks and measurements crisscrossed the walls, a faint promise of plans to come, while a cracked window let in a draft that whispered of needed repairs. Anchoring it all was the brick oven, steadfast and timeless, its presence a quiet reminder of the room's enduring soul. Ryan extended an arm with an exaggerated flourish, a smile tugging at his lips. "And here we have," he said, in the tone of a game show host unveiling a grand prize, "the kitchen of dreams—just waiting for a little TLC."

Mark strolled into the center of the space, spinning slowly like he was inspecting an art gallery exhibit. "So... where's the rest of it? Or does the 'minimalist' thing mean you're eating dinner off a cinder block?"

"Funny," Ryan deadpanned, though a ghost of a smile played on his lips. "That's what the camper is for, Mark. Fully stocked, functional appliances, the whole nine yards." He grinned and gestured toward the kitchen's centerpiece. "And that brick oven? It's staying, no question about it. It's as structurally sound as anything in this house, and a big part of its character. Worst-case scenario, if things get desperate, I'll channel my inner pioneer and cook in there."

Mark crouched slightly, peering at the hearth. "It's not bad. A little elbow grease, maybe a good story, and you've got the heart of the house right here."

Ryan nodded, leaning on a countertop. "That's the plan. Build around what's already good. No sense tearing everything out just to start over."

Mark tilted his head, studying Ryan. "That's not just about houses, is it?"

Ryan shrugged, but the corner of his mouth lifted. "I guess not."

Satisfied with his answer, Mark straightened and ran a hand over the warped countertop beside him. "So, what's the deal with McNeil Construction? Are you turning this project over to the pros?"

"Funny you ask. Got an email from them about an hour ago. They're drawing up a proposal and contract as we speak."

Mark's eyebrows rose. "That's good news. Faith McNeil, working on this house, huh? She doesn't just say yes to anybody, you know."

Ryan tilted his head, smirking. "Are you impressed?"

"Yep," Mark said, grinning. "She's got high standards. So... what'd you think of her? And don't give me the glossy, professional answer. I know you."

Ryan leaned back against the counter and crossed his arms, his smile fading slightly as he considered the question. "She's... impressive. Knows her stuff. Down to earth, but with this no-nonsense edge. You can tell she's had to fight hard as a female in her profession to make her mark."

Mark leaned against the opposite counter, his grin widening as he caught onto a slight hesitance in Ryan's tone. "Color me intrigued. And what else?"

Ryan chuckled softly, shaking his head. "Why do I feel like I'm walking into a trap?"

"Because you are," Mark said, shrugging innocently. "Come on. Honestly, what else?"

Ryan ran a hand over the back of his neck, the rough feel of dust and dirt clinging to his skin. "There's something about her. A kind of... focus. She's edgy... guarded. She doesn't hit me as someone who backs down easily. And I respect that."

"Edgy and guarded? Yeah, that about sums her up," Mark said, drawing out the words with a grin that held far too much amusement for Ryan's liking. "But here's a tip—don't let her rattle you too much. Faith's the kind of woman who can make a grown man twice her size retreat with just a glare. But," he added, his tone softening with a fond chuckle, "she's also the same person who'll slam on the brakes in the middle of Main Street just to escort a turtle safely across the road."

Ryan chuckled. "Noted."

Mark pushed himself off the counter, glancing around the room one last time. "Alright, I think I've fulfilled my civic duty by giving you a hard time today," he said with a sly grin. "So, when am I getting my invitation to bust something up with a sledgehammer?"

Ryan laughed, crossing his arms. "Demolition, huh? Now you're speaking my language. You're welcome anytime. But fair warning—I'll put you to work, and it won't be easy, banker man."

Mark raised an eyebrow, smirking as he strode toward the door. "Oh, I'll work, alright. My price is simple: one large pizza with all the toppings and an endless supply of sweet tea. You think you can swing that?"

"Done," Ryan called after him. "Just let me know when you can tear yourself away from your banker throne."

Pausing at the door, Mark turned, his grin widening. "I'll see what I can do to clear a Saturday."

"Sounds like a plan," Ryan replied, shaking his head with a chuckle.

Mark opened the door but glanced back one last time, his gaze sharp yet filled with that unmistakable hometown camaraderie. "And hey," he said, his voice laced with smooth confidence, "keep dreaming big. Something tells me you've got this. In fact, I think this dream of yours is gonna be great."

Chapter 9

"So," Monica said, sliding into the booth across from Faith at Martha's Diner, "are we going to talk about Ryan Dalton, or are you going to keep pretending he doesn't exist?"

Faith didn't look up from the menu she'd already memorized years ago. "I'm going to pretend you didn't just say that and order the meatloaf special."

"Meatloaf's sold out," Martha called from behind the counter, proving once again that nothing happened in her diner without her knowledge. "But I've got fresh apple pie cooling, and I know that's what you're really here for."

"See?" Faith shot Monica a triumphant look. "We're here for pie."

"We're here," Monica corrected, "because you've been staring at project estimates for the majority of the day, and I decided an intervention was necessary before you permanently fused with your desk chair."

Faith opened her mouth to protest, then closed it again. She had been obsessing over the numbers, trying to make sure the Dalton project would work without stretching their resources or her crew too thin. But that was just good business sense, nothing more.

Martha appeared at their table, coffeepot in hand. Her salt-and-pepper hair escaping its usual neat bun, and her blue eyes sparkled with barely contained curiosity. "You girls decide what you're having? Besides gossip, that is."

"The usual," Monica said. "And maybe a side of information about the Dalton family?"

Faith kicked her under the table, but Martha was already pulling up a chair from a nearby empty table.

"Now there's a name I hadn't heard much until recently," Martha said, filling their coffee cups. "Not since Eleanor passed, God rest her soul. Ryan's back in town, fixing up the old place. He stopped in for coffee the other mornin'."

"He's trying to," Faith muttered into her coffee.

"Trying being the operative word," Monica added with a grin. "Faith just did the initial walk-through today."

Martha's eyes lit up. "Did he show you Eleanor's kitchen? That brick oven of hers made the best bread in three counties. Used to trade me her sourdough starters for fresh produce from my garden." She shook her head, smiling at the memory. "That whole family had a way of making you feel so loved and welcomed, even if you were just stopping by to deliver the mail."

Faith found herself leaning forward. "You knew them well?"

"Honey, everyone knew the Daltons. Frank and Eleanor were fixtures here before they passed on. And Ryan? Lord, that boy followed his grandparents around everywhere they went."

"Really?" Faith tried to imagine a younger Ryan, probably all gangly limbs and that same eager smile.

"Mm-hmm. Always had his nose in some book about buildings or business. Wanted to know how everything worked, that one. His grandfather encouraged it, too. Used to say Ryan had an old soul in young hands."

The image struck something in Faith's memory. "I think... I remember him, actually, now that I think about it. He helped my dad once when our delivery truck broke down. Must have been, what, fifteen years ago?"

Martha nodded enthusiastically. "That sounds like Ryan. Always ready to lend a hand, even if he didn't know exactly what he was doing yet. His heart was in the right place, though."

"Still is, apparently," Monica said pointedly. "Even if his renovation skills may need some work."

"That house needs a lot of TLC," Faith sighed, giving up the pretense of studying the menu. "The repairs alone... and he wants to do some of it himself. With YouTube tutorials and books."

Martha's laugh was warm and knowing. "Sounds like his grandfather. Frank always said you learn best by doing. Course, he also said measuring once and praying twice was the best way to do everything in life. And... Ryan really is a fine young man, and handsome to boot."

"See?" Monica gestured triumphantly with her coffee cup. "It's meant to be. The project, I mean."

"The project," Faith repeated firmly, ignoring the way Martha and Monica exchanged knowing looks. "Which is complicated enough without you two turning it into some kind of small-town romance novel."

"Who said anything about romance?" Martha's innocent tone wouldn't have fooled a kindergartner. "Ryan sure did grow up to be an awful pretty man, though. Those Dalton men all had good shoulders. Must be from all that hard work."

Faith dropped her head into her hands. "Can we please talk about something else? Anything else?"

"Fine." Monica's voice was suspiciously agreeable. "Let's talk about how you're going to handle working closely with him for the next several weeks, probably months, actually. Purely professionally, of course."

"Of course," Martha echoed. "Just like how Frank and Eleanor started out 'purely professionally' when she hired his construction company to renovate her father's store."

Faith's head snapped up. "What?"

"Oh, didn't you know?" Martha's smile was downright mischievous now. "That's how they met. Eleanor inherited her father's hardware store and hired Frank to modernize it. Six months later, they were engaged. Said they fell in love watching something old become something new again."

"That's..." Faith struggled to find words that wouldn't encourage them. "Not relevant to anything."

"Course not," Martha agreed cheerfully, heading toward the kitchen. "Just like it's not relevant that Ryan has his grandmother's eyes. Or that God led him to McNeil Construction, even though there are three other contractors in the county."

Faith turned to Monica as Martha disappeared through the swinging doors. "A little help here?"

"Sorry." Monica was clearly trying not to laugh. "But you have to admit, it's kind of perfect. The prodigal grandson returns home, hires the talented local contractor..."

"Stop," Faith interrupted. "The story stops right there. The contracts not signed yet. I can still change my mind."

"But you won't." Monica's voice softened, turning serious. "Faith, I saw the preliminary numbers you were working on. This project is exactly what the company needs right now, especially with the medical bills piling up. And you, my friend, need to dig into this project and use it as a distraction. Something to focus on while your daddy focuses on getting better."

The reminder of her dad's health sobered Faith's irritation. She stared into her coffee cup, watching the light play across its surface. "It's risky. If anything goes wrong, if he runs out of money halfway through..."

"Then you'll figure it out. You always do." Monica reached across the table, squeezing Faith's hand. "And maybe, just maybe, you'll let someone else help figure things out, too."

"I have you for that," Faith pointed out.

"You do. And now you might have someone else too. Someone who looks at old houses the same way you do—like they're full of life waiting to be lived."

Faith was saved from responding by Martha's return with their food. The conversation shifted to safer topics: town gossip, upcoming projects, Monica's latest dating disaster. But Faith's mind kept drifting back to the Dalton farmhouse, to its solid bones and hidden potential.

And maybe, just maybe, to the way Ryan's eyes had lit up when he talked about his grandmother's kitchen.

"You're thinking about it again," Monica said smugly, cutting into her chicken fried steak.

"I'm thinking about the logistics," Faith said. "The timeline, the budget, the crew assignments..."

"The way he filled out those new work boots?"

Faith pointed her fork accusingly. "That's it. No pie for you."

Martha's laugh carried across the diner. "Don't worry, honey. I've got plenty of pie. And plenty of stories about young Ryan Dalton, if you're interested."

"I'm not," Faith insisted, even as her traitorous mind filed away everything Martha had shared about the Daltons. It was just research, she told herself. Background information on a potential client. Nothing more.

But later, as she drove home through Laurel Ridge's quiet streets, Faith found herself taking the long way, the very out of the way route home that led past the Dalton farmhouse. The house appeared to have every light on. She could almost picture Ryan surrounded by renovation books and building plans, that determined look on his face as he tackled another YouTube tutorial.

"Just a job," she muttered to herself. "That's all it is."

The late evening breeze carried the scent of spring through her open window. Somewhere in the distance, a church bell tolled, its sound carrying across the valley like a reminder of things past and possibilities ahead.

Faith turned up her radio, drowning out both the bells and her own thoughts. She had estimates to finalize, crews to coordinate, and a father's recovery to worry about. Romance was a luxury she couldn't afford, no matter how many charming stories Martha had about renovations leading to relationships.

Besides, she told herself firmly, anyone who thought YouTube tutorials were an adequate preparation for historical restoration clearly needed their head examined. Even if he did have his grandmother's eyes.

Faith focused on the road ahead, pretending she couldn't see the Dalton farmhouse's silhouette in her rearview mirror, standing proud against the darkening sky like a challenge waiting to be accepted.

Or maybe, whispered a voice that sounded suspiciously like Monica's, like a life waiting to be lived.

Chapter 10

Faith clutched her project folder like a shield as she approached the Dalton farmhouse. The morning air was crisp with early spring, and she could hear hammering coming from somewhere inside. Apparently, Ryan was already hard at work—or at least attempting to be.

She found him in the kitchen, surrounded by what appeared to be the remains of a cabinet door. His dark hair was dusted with wood particles, and he was frowning at his phone, probably watching another tutorial. Faith cleared her throat.

"Please tell me that wasn't a load-bearing cabinet."

Ryan looked up, relief washing over his features. "Faith! No, just trying to remove some of the seventy's horror show. Though I'm starting to think I should've waited for the experts."

He gestured at the splintered wood around him, and Faith bit back a smile. "Starting to?"

"Okay, I definitely should have waited on a few things." Ryan ran a hand through his hair, sending up a small cloud of dust. "But in my defense, the YouTube guy made it look really easy."

"The YouTube guy probably wasn't dealing with oak cabinets that have been painted over six times." Faith set her folder on a relatively clean corner of the counter. "Which is why we're going to discuss terms and conditions before you demolish anything else, and I agree to take on this project."

Ryan straightened, brushing dust from his shirt in a futile attempt to look more professional. "Right. The contract. Let me just..." He glanced around at the debris. "Maybe we should move this conversation somewhere less destructive?"

Faith nodded, following him to the library. The room was notably untouched by renovation attempts, though she noticed he'd cleared a space near the window, setting up a folding table and chairs. Morning light filtered through the dusty windows, catching the planes of his face as he sat down and gestured to her to do the same.

Faith firmly redirected her attention to her folder.

"First things first," she said, pulling out the contract. "This outlines the scope of work, timeline, and payment schedule. We'll focus on the structural elements—foundation repair, porch reconstruction, roof replacement, which I'm sure we will bring in another contractor for, and updating all mechanical systems. Your DIY projects will need to work around our schedule."

Ryan accepted the document, scanning the pages. "Seems reasonable. Though I notice you've included the library bookcases in your scope."

"Non-negotiable." Faith crossed her arms. "You're not touching that quarter-sawn oak with a heat gun, YouTube tutorial or not."

"Fair enough." Ryan's lips twitched. "Though I did manage to strip paint in Chicago without burning down my condo."

"Congratulations. Was it also irreplaceable nineteenth-century craftsmanship?"

"Point taken." He continued reading, and Faith found herself studying his profile, the way his brow furrowed slightly in concentration. She quickly looked away when he glanced up. "The timeline seems aggressive."

"It needs to be. Summer's coming, and I want the exterior work done before the weather turns unbearably hot."

Ryan chuckled. "Makes sense."

"Why a B&B?" she asked before she could stop herself. "You could flip this place, make a decent profit once it's restored."

Ryan was quiet for a moment, his expression thoughtful. "You ever have a place that just... feels like home? Not because you grew up there, necessarily, but because something about it speaks to who you are?"

"Maybe."

"This is home for me," Ryan continued. "I grew up on the other side of Laurel Ridge in a house. My parents were good people, but they were academics—always thinking, always working, always on the move to climb another ladder in life, focused on their research. But here... in this home? With my grandparents? This is where I learned to build things, to work with my hands. I learned how to live here, truly live a life of adventure and wonder and purpose. This is where I learned what love is. This is where I figured out who I wanted to be, even if it took me a while to get there."

Faith found she couldn't look away from the earnestness in his eyes. "I want to share that. Create a place where people can step back, breathe, maybe find a piece of themselves they forgot existed. I want everyone to feel welcomed when they come here and leave their worries at the front door. Does that sound crazy?"

"Yes," Faith said honestly. "But also... kind of perfect."

Their eyes held for a moment too long. Faith cleared her throat, turning back to the contract. "You'll need updated insurance coverage before we begin. And we should discuss the payment schedule."

"Already handled the insurance." Ryan produced a folder of his own. "And I can work with whatever schedule works best for your cash flow. I know restoration projects can be unpredictable."

Faith blinked, surprised by his forethought. "That's... unusually accommodating."

"I did work in finance," he reminded her with a grin. "I understand the importance of maintaining good working relationships. Besides, my grandfather would come back to haunt me if I caused problems for James McNeil's daughter."

"You remember my father?"

"Your dad and my grandfather—two men who taught half the contractors in this county. They worked together on so many projects, trading skills and knowledge along the way." Ryan's expression softened. "How's he doing? I heard he's been unwell."

Faith tensed, her professional mask slipping back into place. "He's recovering. Now, about the timeline—"

"Faith." Ryan's voice was gentle, but firm. "I know you're trying to keep this strictly professional. But we're going to be working together for months, probably driving each other crazy with different opinions about everything from paint colors to porch railings. Maybe we could try being friends too?"

"Friends don't generally pay friends hundreds of thousands of dollars for construction work," Faith pointed out.

"True. But friends can appreciate that sometimes life gets complicated, and maybe having someone to talk to isn't the worst thing in the world."

Faith studied him, trying to find the angle, the hidden agenda. But all she saw was genuine concern and that same earnestness that seemed to radiate from him like warmth from an old brick fireplace.

"Let's start with getting through this contract," she said finally. "Then we can discuss the complexities of contractor-client relationships."

Ryan's smile suggested he recognized the deflection, but was willing to let it slide. "Deal. Though I reserve the right to bring you coffee when you're yelling at me about proper restoration techniques."

"I don't yell," Faith protested. "I express professional concern. Firmly."

"Of course." Ryan's eyes danced with amusement. "My mistake. Now, about these contract details..."

They spent the next hour going through the contract line by line. Faith was impressed despite herself—Ryan asked intelligent questions, understood the technical requirements, and seemed genuinely interested in learning about proper restoration methods. His enthusiasm was almost contagious, though Faith maintained her professional distance.

Almost.

"No," she said firmly, pointing to a particular clause. "You cannot be on site during major demolition work. It's a liability issue."

"Even if I promise to wear a hard hat and look devastatingly handsome in it?"

Faith refused to acknowledge the way her stomach flipped at his teasing grin. "Even then. Besides, you'll be busy enough with your own projects, some of which I'm sure you can do in that barn outside... away from danger. Speaking of which..." She pulled out another document. "These are the ground rules for your DIY adventures."

Ryan accepted the papers, eyebrows rising as he read. "No power tools before 7 AM or after 10 PM? I'm wounded by your lack of faith in my consideration."

"The neighbors will thank me. And so will you, once you realize how much work you've taken on."

"Probably," he admitted. "Though I'm starting to think I might need more than books, online guides, and YouTube tutorials."

Faith hesitated, then made a decision she hoped she wouldn't regret. "I could... show you a few basics if you get stuck. Proper techniques for stripping woodwork, that sort of thing. Just to prevent any disasters."

Ryan's face lit up. "Really? That would be amazing. I promise to be a model student."

"We'll see about that." Faith said, trying to ignore how pleased he looked. "I'll have Monica draw up the final contract this morning. We can start work tomorrow, as long as you come by the office later this afternoon and sign the contract."

"I'll sign." Ryan said as he walked her to the door. "Thank you, Faith. Not just for taking this huge job on, but for being willing to let me handle some of the renovations on my own. I know I'm not the typical client."

"No," Faith agreed, pausing and turning to face him on the porch. "You're definitely not typical."

Something shifted in Ryan's expression, a warmth that made Faith's pulse skip. She quickly stepped back, maintaining professional distance.

"Contract... this afternoon. Come sign it," she said briskly. "My crew and I will be here first thing in the morning tomorrow. Try not to demolish everything in sight."

Ryan's laugh followed her down the steps. "No promises. But I'll try to save the real destruction for when the experts are here to witness it."

Faith shook her head, but she couldn't quite suppress her smile as she walked to her truck. This project was either going to be the best decision she'd ever made, or the most complicated few months of her life.

Possibly both.

The thought should have worried her more than it did. Instead, she found herself looking forward to tomorrow, to the challenge of bringing this old house back to life. And, if she had to be honest, she was also looking forward to watching Ryan learn the difference between YouTube tutorials and reality... well, that was just a professional interest in a client's development.

Nothing more.

Right.

Chapter 11

"Alright, let's make this count." Faith stood in the driveway of the Dalton farmhouse, surrounded by her crew, as the morning fog lifted from the mountains. "Tom, get the scaffolding set up on the east side. We'll start with the structural assessment of the porch roof. Mike, I want you and Steve to inspect the foundation around the house, mark anything that stands out as an issue."

Tom nodded, already directing the crew members toward the equipment truck. "What about our enthusiastic homeowner? He planning to supervise?"

Faith caught the skepticism in Tom's tone. "Mr. Dalton knows to stay clear of the major work areas. According to what he told me, he'll be focusing on the kitchen today."

"Yeah? With his YouTube degree in renovation?" Tom's weathered face creased with doubt. "Hope he knows which end of a hammer to hold."

"He'll be fine," Faith said, more defensively than she'd intended. "And he's willing to admit when he needs help. Cut him some slack, Tom."

"Speaking of help…" Tom gestured toward the back of the house, where Ryan was unloading lumber from his truck.

Faith bit back a smile. "Just get the scaffolding started, please."

She walked across the yard, her eyes on Ryan as he grappled with an awkward stack of boards.

"Need a hand?"

Ryan looked up. "Is it that obvious? Do I look helpless?"

"No, just thought I'd offer a hand. But do me a favor and carry lumber this way, or you'll throw your back out."

"I never knew there was a right or a wrong way to carry lumber," Ryan said, grinning as Faith demonstrated. "Though I have to admit, learning from you is much more effective than a YouTube video."

Faith stepped back, maintaining professional distance. "Just remember to lift with your legs, not your back. And try not to drop anything on your feet. Those boots might be new, but they're not indestructible."

"Noted." Ryan glanced at the activity in the yard. "Your crew seems efficient."

"They're the best." Faith watched Tom directing the scaffolding setup with practiced ease. "And they know what they're doing, so—"

"Stay out of their way?" Ryan finished. "Don't worry, I plan to focus on my kitchen disaster today. Speaking of which…" He hesitated. "I might have discovered a slight plumbing situation that needs attention."

Faith's eyes narrowed. "Define situation."

"Remember that cabinet I was removing yesterday?" Ryan led her toward the back door to the kitchen, talking faster. "Well, it turns out there might have been a reason it was installed at that weird angle. It appears the access to the main water line..."

Faith followed him into the kitchen, where a steady drip echoed from behind a partially demolished wall. "Ryan."

"I know, I know. I should have checked for pipes before starting the demo." He ran a hand through his hair, making it stand up slightly. "In my defense, the YouTube guy didn't mention—"

"If you say 'YouTube guy' one more time, I'm doubling my hourly rate." Faith knelt to examine the pipe, which was indeed showing signs of age and stress. "Hand me that wrench."

Ryan complied, watching as Faith assessed the damage. "How bad is it?"

"Could be worse." Faith tested the pipe's connection, frowning at the corrosion. "But this whole section needs to be replaced before we go any further. Someone did some creative plumbing that wouldn't pass inspection today."

"Can you fix it?"

"Of course, I can fix it." Faith sat back on her heels, mentally calculating materials and time. "But it means adjusting today's schedule. And you owe me coffee for the next week."

"Deal." Ryan's relief was palpable. "How did you get into this? Construction, I mean. It's not exactly a common career choice for..."

"For a woman?" Faith's tone carried a warning edge.

"For anyone, really," Ryan corrected smoothly. "I mean, most kids don't grow up dreaming about plumbing repairs and structural engineering. Though watching you work, maybe they should. I mean, I get it... my dream as a kid was to work with my hands and follow in my grandfather's footsteps..."

Faith found herself softening slightly at his genuine interest. "I grew up in it. Dad started teaching me basic carpentry as soon as I could hold a hammer. It just... made sense to me. Wood, tools, the way things fit together."

"Like a puzzle?"

"Yeah, something like that, but kind of more like a story." Faith surprised herself with the admission. "Every house has one, if you know how to read it. The way it was built, the choices people made, the lives that shaped it."

Ryan's eyes lit with understanding. "That's exactly how I feel about this place. Every room holds memories. Every room can tell a story. I want to honor that, you know?"

Faith did know. It was the same feeling she got working on historical renovations, preserving craftsmanship that deserved to be remembered.

"So... could you expand a bit on what you mentioned earlier?" she asked.

"Expand on what?"

"Your childhood dream," she said, her eyes studying him intently.

"Oh, that," he replied, a trace of nostalgia flickering in his tone. "When I was a kid, I always thought I'd grow up to work alongside my grandfather—learn from him, soak in all his knowledge. Maybe one day, I'd even take over his company."

"And how did you go from dreaming of becoming a construction worker to ending up in finance?" she asked.

"Let's just say my parents had bigger plans for me. They were set on me going to college, getting a degree, and chasing the so-called American dream. I followed their advice, and for a while, it paid off—until it didn't," he replied.

"That must have been tough—having academic parents pushing you toward something that didn't align with what you really wanted," she said.

"It was tough," he admitted. "But, you know, it is what it is. I wanted to make them proud, and for a time, I did. It just... wasn't the right fit for me in the end."

A crash from outside broke the moment. Faith jumped up. "I should check on the crew."

"Right, of course." Ryan stepped back, giving her space.

Chapter 12

The plumbing repair took longer than expected, involving not just pipe replacement, but also discovering and fixing several questionable modifications made in the past. Ryan hovered nearby, asking intelligent questions and actually taking notes instead of reaching for his phone to look up tutorials.

"Whoever did this clearly learned their trade from a cereal box," Faith muttered, wrestling with a particularly stubborn joint.

"Well, I can guarantee this wasn't done by my grandfather. He would have never rigged the plumbing this way," Ryan said.

"Well, at least you didn't attempt to fix this yourself." Faith sat back, wiping sweat from her forehead. "Plumbing really isn't too difficult to figure out, though. Not if you think of it like putting a puzzle together. You probably could have figured some of this out yourself, but better safe than sorry."

"Speaking from experience?"

"Let's just say there's a reason I handle all the plumbing repairs at Dad's house now. He can't stand plumbing work." Faith tightened the final connection, then tested the water pressure. "There. That should hold until we can do a proper renovation of the whole system."

"My hero," Ryan said solemnly, then ducked as Faith threw a rag at his head. "I mean, thank you for your professional assistance with this unforeseen circumstance."

"Better." Faith gathered her tools, trying not to smile. "Though next time, maybe check for pipes before you start swinging a sledgehammer?"

"What, and miss out on quality time with my favorite contractor?"

Faith told herself the warmth in her chest was just from the physical work. "I'm your only contractor."

"Semantics." Ryan said as he helped her clean up the workspace. "Seriously, though, thank you. I know this wasn't on today's schedule."

"It's fine. Renovation projects always have surprises." Faith straightened, stretching muscles tired from hours of awkward positions. "Though usually not on the first day."

"I like to be exceptional," Ryan said with a grin that made her stomach flip. "Keeps things interesting."

"Interesting is certainly one way to describe it," she said with a small smile, her tone laced with curiosity. "So, tell me—what exactly do you envision for the kitchen? You mentioned wanting to modernize it a bit, but also keeping some of its original character. I'm intrigued. What details are you thinking of preserving? And how do you imagine blending the old with the new? Walk me through your vision—I'd love to hear more."

Ryan leaned against the counter, his expression thoughtful as he considered her question. "Well, for starters, I can't imagine getting rid of the old farmhouse sink. It's beat up, sure, but there's history there. I remember my grandma washing tons of apples and garden produce in that sink. I guess it feels…rooted, you know? Like it belongs here. I can still picture her cleaning produce, getting it all ready to preserve."

Faith nodded slowly, her eyes scanning the sink behind him. "Vintage sinks like this can be a centerpiece, actually. If we refinish it and pair it with the right fixtures, it could really shine. What else?"

"The cabinets—or at least some of them," Ryan said, gesturing toward the faded wooden frames lining the room. "They're old, no doubt about it, but there's something about their imperfections that I find… fun, I guess. Too many memories tied to them to just throw them away. My great-grandfather built these, you know. I'm thinking of upgrading the kitchen with stainless-steel appliances and quartz countertops. Some of these old cabinets will go out to the barn. I want to expand the workshop area out there and give them a second life. For the kitchen, though, I think durable oak cabinets with some character will suit the space much better."

Faith smirked. "Sounds like you're aiming for a modern kitchen with soul."

"Exactly," Ryan said, brightening. "And as much as I like the original features, I don't want the place to feel like it's stuck in time. It needs to work with how people live now—open, light, usable. Like, I've always pictured a big island in the middle here, something that brings people together instead of keeping them in separate corners."

Faith could picture it, all of it. Despite his inexperience, it was clear that he cared about this place, not just for himself, but for the stories etched into its bones. It made her want to meet him halfway, to take his raw ideas and shape them into something tangible.

"An island could work," she said, tilting her head as she mentally rearranged the space. "We might have to adjust the layout of the kitchen a bit. Might have to reroute the plumbing. Definitely need more electrical outlets. Maybe swap out some upper cabinets for open shelving, something sleek but rustic at the same time, so the island doesn't feel boxed in. What do you think?"

Ryan's mouth lifted at the corners. "I think you're really good at this."

Faith rolled her eyes, though she couldn't hide the satisfaction in her voice. "Alright, don't start buttering me up. You need to think about your budget before you get attached to any of these ideas."

"Budget, right, of course," Ryan said, straightening with mock seriousness. "I'll keep it realistic...ish. Within reason."

"Good thing I've already got a healthy skepticism about your definition of 'reason.'"

"Sounds like you're ready to join me on the kitchen renovation," he said with a hopeful smile. "I think working on this space together will be a lot more fun than tackling it on my own."

She laughed and replied, "And here I was, accidentally signing up for extra work without even realizing it."

He grinned mischievously. "Just remember, the main bedroom and the library are still my domains—no trespassing."

"Except for those built-in shelves in the library," she shot back with a playful smirk. "Those are all mine to handle. Don't forget it."

He laughed. They stood together in the stillness of the kitchen, dust lingering in the air and half-repaired walls framing the space. Yet, it felt alive—like it was already shedding its weary past and leaning toward something fresh and full of promise.

Faith turned and made her way to the door, suddenly needing space from his easy charm and the unfairly distracting way he managed to make a work shirt look better than any financial analyst ever should. "I should check on the progress outside."

"Faith?" Ryan's voice stopped her. "I mean this sincerely. Thanks for not making me feel completely incompetent. Even though we both know I am."

"You're not incompetent," Faith said before she could stop herself. "Just…"

"Enthusiastically naïve?"

"Something like that," Faith said with a grin. "But in a good way. You're learning, and there's nothing wrong with that."

The look of pleasure on Ryan's face was almost worth the admission. Almost.

The rest of the day flew by in a whirlwind of activity. By sunset, the scaffolding was firmly in place, the foundation inspection had been signed off, and Faith's crew had made considerable headway in assessing the porch's structural flaws. Meanwhile, Ryan had steered clear of any additional plumbing mishaps. As for Faith, she had skillfully kept her distance from Ryan, determined to maintain her professional poise and keep her attention firmly fixed on the task at hand.

"Good first day," Tom admitted grudgingly as they packed up tools. "Though tomorrows when the real work starts."

Faith nodded, watching Ryan chat with Mike about proper demolition techniques. "He's not what you expected, is he?"

"He's something, all right." Tom's expression was knowing. "Just remember, boss—mixing business with pleasure can get complicated."

"There's no mixing," Faith said firmly. "This is strictly professional."

"Sure it is." Tom's skepticism was clear. "That's why you spent two hours fixing his plumbing instead of delegating it to Steve."

"That was just…" Faith searched for a professional-sounding explanation. "Quality control."

"Right." Tom shouldered his tool belt. "Well, whatever you want to call it, try not to let it interfere with the actual work. We've got a tight schedule to keep. Remember that."

Faith watched him head for his truck, irritation warring with the uncomfortable knowledge that he might have a point.

"Faith?" Ryan approached, looking somehow more appealing with sawdust in his hair and honest fatigue on his face. "Everything okay?"

"Fine," she said quickly. "Just running through tomorrow's schedule in my mind. Trying to be realistic about what my crew can accomplish."

"Ah." Ryan nodded sagely. "Planning how to prevent any disasters?"

Despite herself, Faith smiled. "Something like that."

"Well, I promise to consult actual humans before attempting any more major demolition." Ryan's expression turned serious. "I really do appreciate everything you're doing here. Letting me do some of the work myself instead of just being the guy writing checks."

Faith met his eyes, finding nothing but sincerity in their hazel depths. "You're not just the guy writing checks, Ryan. This is your home. Your legacy. That matters. I get it."

Something shifted in Ryan's expression that made Faith's pulse skip. She quickly looked away, gesturing to her truck.

"I should go. Early start tomorrow."

"Right." Ryan stepped back, but his smile remained. "Same time tomorrow? I'll have the coffee ready."

"Just try not to break anything major before I get here," Faith called over her shoulder, already heading for her escape route.

Ryan's laugh followed her to the truck. "No promises!"

Chapter 13

F aith balanced two Styrofoam to-go coffee cups as she navigated the familiar hall through Mercy Regional Medical Center's cardiac wing. The evening shift nurses offered tired smiles as she passed.

"There she is," Nancy, her father's favorite nurse, called out. "Right on schedule."

"Traffic was light." Faith said. "How's he doing today?"

"Restless. Been watching old westerns all afternoon and evening, pretending he's not counting the hours until he can go home." Nancy's expression softened. "He misses work."

"And I miss him being there," Faith muttered, though she knew her father's restlessness went deeper than simple boredom. James McNeil had never been good at sitting still, even before his heart decided to remind them all of his mortality.

She found him exactly as Nancy had described, staring at the TV, where John Wayne was facing down some nameless villain. Her father's reading glasses sat on the bedside table, along with what looked like old paperwork he'd hastily shoved aside.

"I brought reinforcements," Faith announced, holding up the coffee cups. "Decaf, just as the doctor ordered."

James brightened, reaching for the cup with hands that looked too thin against the hospital blanket on his lap. "Martha's?"

"Of course. Accept no substitutes." Faith settled into the vinyl chair beside his bed, trying not to notice how the medical machinery and gadgets threw harsh shadows across his face. "Martha told me to tell you that you'd better hurry up and get back to your regular booth. She misses seeing you every morning."

Her father's chuckle turned into a slight cough, and Faith pretended not to notice how he pressed a hand against his chest. "I miss her too—she's such a wonderful woman. Always so cheerful, such a vibrant personality. So, how are things at the office? How's the Dalton project coming along?"

"Not bad, it's going fine." Faith took a deliberate sip of coffee, avoiding her father's too-perceptive gaze.

"Mm hmm. Any major hiccups yet?"

"No, nothing major. We are still right on schedule, mostly." Faith launched into a detailed update about the porch reconstruction, foundation repairs, and the endless permit paperwork. Shop talk was safe territory, familiar ground where they both knew the rules.

Her father listened with the focused attention he'd always given her project reports, asking specific questions about load-bearing calculations and material choices. But something felt off about his interest, as if he was using the conversation to avoid something else.

"The original joists are in better shape than we expected," Faith concluded, watching him carefully. "Though we'll still need to—Dad? What is it?"

James abruptly shifted, snapping shut the notebook resting beside him on the bed near his tablet. Faith managed to catch a fleeting glimpse of what appeared to be a chaotic mix of scribbled notes and ear-marked pages.

"Nothing important," he said too quickly. "Now, about those joists—"

"Dad." Faith set down her coffee. "What aren't you telling me?"

"Faith, can we not talk about what's on my mind right now?" he said. "Did you bring the files from the office like I asked?"

"I get the feeling you aren't telling me something."

James sighed, his expression turning serious. "Faith, honey... we need to talk about the business. About what happens if—"

"No." Faith stood abruptly, her chair scraping against the linoleum. "We are not having this conversation. You're going to get better, and everything will go back to normal."

"You sound just like your mother sometimes," James said. "So stubborn about facing things you don't want to see."

The comment hit like a physical blow. Faith turned away, pretending to study the sunset through the window while she got her expression under control. "Mom ran away from everything. I'm still here."

"Faith—"

A knock at the door interrupted whatever he'd been about to say. Dr. Benson entered, her white coat pristine despite the late hour. "Evening, McNeil family. How are we feeling today, James?"

Faith watched as her father straightened slightly, putting on what she thought of as his 'client meeting' face. "Right as rain, Doc. When can I get back to work?"

"Let's look at your latest test results first." Dr. Benson pulled up something on her tablet, but Faith noticed how her father made a subtle gesture, almost imperceptible. The doctor's expression didn't change, but she angled the screen away from Faith's view.

"Blood pressure's still higher than we'd like," Dr. Benson continued smoothly. "And the new medication doesn't seem to be—"

"What aren't you telling me?" Faith interrupted, looking between her father and the doctor. "And don't say nothing."

"Faith." Her father's voice carried a warning. "Dr. Benson is just being thorough."

"No, she's being careful. There's a difference." Faith crossed her arms. "I'm not a child, Dad. I think I can handle whatever it is that's going on."

A heavy silence filled the room. Dr. Benson glanced at James, who shook his head slightly.

"I'll let you two talk," the doctor said diplomatically. "We can discuss the test results tomorrow morning, James."

Faith waited until the door closed behind her before turning back to her father. "Seriously? You're sending signals to the doctor, thinking I won't notice?"

"It's not what you think."

"Really? Because what I think is that you're hiding something from me. Something about your health, something to do with that notebook and all these files you keep asking me to bring you."

"Faith." James reached for her hand, his grip surprisingly strong. "Sit down. Please."

She dropped back into the chair, suddenly exhausted. "Just... tell me what's going on. Please."

Her father was quiet for a long moment, studying their joined hands. Faith noticed absently that she still had dirt and sawdust under her nails from the day's work. Her father noticed too, a slight smile touching his lips.

"Remember your first summer helping on a job site?" he asked unexpectedly. "You were so determined to carry lumber like the grown-ups, even though the boards were twice your size."

"Dad—"

"You got more splinters than actual work done," he continued, his voice soft with memory. "But you never complained. Just kept coming back, day after day, until you figured it out."

"That's different. I was learning something new. This is—"

"This is me trying to protect you," James interrupted. "Maybe for too long."

Faith's chest tightened with sudden fear. "Protect me from what?"

Her father looked away, his gaze falling on the notebook. "Some things... some truths are like old houses, Faith. Sometimes the foundation isn't what you thought it was. And sometimes it's better to shore things up before you start uncovering problems."

"Dad, you're starting to sound like those renovation shows you hate."

He managed a weak chuckle. "Maybe they're not all nonsense." His expression turned serious again. "I need you to just trust me. Can you do that?"

Faith wanted to argue, wanted to demand answers about his health, about the files he kept asking she bring, about all the things that felt increasingly wrong. But something in his face stopped her—a mixture of love and worry that made her throat tight.

"Fine," she said finally. "But this conversation isn't over."

"I know." He squeezed her hand again. "Now, tell me more about the Dalton renovation."

Faith recognized the deliberate change of subject, but let it pass. She launched into a detailed description of the porch reconstruction, watching her father slowly relax as she talked about proper joint angles and weather-resistant materials.

Later, sitting in her truck in the dark parking lot, Faith pulled out her phone to check messages. Three from Monica, and one from Tom about next week's work schedule.

Despite everything, Faith smiled as she read through Monica's texts. She started to type a response, then stopped, as her phone buzzed with another incoming text from her:

"Girl whining session tomorrow night? I'll bring pizza, you bring your problems. No construction talk allowed."

Faith sent back a quick agreement, then dropped her phone into the passenger seat. The hospital loomed in front of her, its windows lit like tired eyes in the darkness. Somewhere in there, her father was probably already looking through the file folders she had brought him that he had requested, carrying whatever burden he thought she couldn't handle.

She started her truck, the familiar rumble oddly comforting. Tomorrow she'd worry about all the things her father wasn't telling her. Tonight, she just wanted to go home and lose herself in the simple pleasure of working on her latest personal project, a bookcase, letting the rhythm of sanding and measuring drown out all the questions she wasn't ready to face.

The moon hung low over the mountains as Faith drove home, painting the familiar roads in shades of silver and shadow. In her mind, she could still feel her father's grip on her hand, still see the worry in his eyes when he talked about foundations and truth.

Some problems couldn't be fixed with a saw and level, no matter how much she wished they could.

Chapter 14

The bell above Earl's Hardware's front door chimed as Faith entered, bringing with it the familiar smell of lumber, metal, and the coffee Earl Jr. perpetually had brewing behind the counter. The store hadn't changed since she was a kid—same worn wooden floors, same carefully organized shelves, same feeling of possibility in every aisle.

"If it isn't my favorite contractor," Earl called out from his perch behind the register. "Don't you ever take a day off?"

"Just picking up a few things for a personal project," Faith said.

"Personal project?" Earl replied, a knowing grin spreading across his face.

"A bookcase I've been building," she explained.

"Impressive," Earl said with a raised eyebrow. "You're always up to something, aren't you? How's your dad doing, by the way? I sure miss swapping stories with him."

"He's doing alright, Earl. Thanks for asking," she replied.

"Have they said anything about when he might be able to come home?"

"Not yet, but I'm hoping it won't be too much longer," she said.

"I think I'll head up to the hospital after I close up today. It's been too long—I miss my buddy," he said.

"Well, Earl, I know Daddy would love to see you. It might just lift his spirits," she said, making her way down the aisle toward the specialty hardware section of the store.

She turned the corner and found Ryan surrounded by what looked like every white paint sample in the store, his expression a perfect mix of confusion and determination.

"Having trouble choosing a color?" she asked as she approached.

Ryan startled, dropping several samples. "Faith! Thank goodness. Please tell me you can explain the difference between 'Cloud White' and 'Whisper White' because I've been staring at these for twenty minutes, and they're all just... white."

"That's because you're holding about fifty shades of it." Faith picked up a fallen sample. "Maybe it's time to branch out. Consider something radical like... beige."

"Hilarious." Ryan gathered the scattered samples. "I thought white would be safe for the bedrooms, but apparently, there are more varieties of white than there are tools in this store."

"Not quite, but it's close." Faith studied the samples in his hands. "What are you trying to achieve? Warm? Cool? Modern? Traditional?"

"Yes?" Ryan's sheepish grin was oddly endearing. "I just want the rooms to feel welcoming. Like somewhere people can relax and feel at home."

Something about his earnest tone made Faith soften. "Okay, first lesson in paint selection: put down everything with 'whisper' in the name. Those are marketing gimmicks. Let's look at the undertones."

She spent the next few minutes explaining the subtle differences between warm and cool whites, watching Ryan's confusion gradually transform into understanding. He asked intelligent questions about light reflection and how different times of day would affect the color, taking notes on his phone.

"You're actually getting better at this," Faith admitted, helping him narrow down the choices to three options.

"High praise from the master craftswoman herself." Ryan tucked the winning samples into his pocket. "Though I'm still learning. Yesterday, I watched three different YouTube videos about proper paint roller techniques."

"Progress. At least you're not trying to learn major demolition from the internet anymore."

"Hey, that cabinet had it coming." Ryan said. "Working on something special today?"

"A bookcase," she said. "I've run out of space to store books in my office in my apartment."

"Apartment?" he replied, surprised. "I pictured you living in a beautifully restored house... one you renovated yourself, of course."

"Not yet," she chuckled. "I haven't found the perfect house that feels like home. For now, I'm living in an apartment above my dad's garage. It's actually close to McNeil headquarters. It just makes sense—it's affordable, and I get to be near my dad."

"That's nice," he said. "How's your dad holding up?"

"He's doing alright," she replied. "I stopped by the hospital yesterday after leaving your place. Honestly, he just wants to be home. And I'm more than ready to have him back."

"You really miss having him around, huh?"

Faith met his eyes, finding nothing but genuine concern there. "I miss him everywhere, at home, at work," she admitted quietly. "Even here. He bought me my first real tool set from this store when I was eight. I thought it meant I could fix anything."

"Maybe you can." Ryan's smile was soft. "From what I've seen, you're not far off."

A comfortable silence fell between them, broken only by the distant sound of Earl helping another customer. Faith realized she'd been in the store far longer than she had intended, but somehow couldn't make herself move away.

"Have you eaten?" Ryan asked suddenly. "I was thinking of heading to Martha's. A good home cooked breakfast sounds really good."

She should say no. She had the bookcase to finish, paperwork to review, a dozen reasons to maintain professional distance.

"Martha's biscuits and gravy are pretty spectacular."

Ryan's whole face lit up. "Is that a yes?"

"That's a 'you're buying since I just saved you from a paint disaster.'"

"Deal." Ryan followed her to the register, where Earl was doing a poor job of hiding his interest in their conversation. "Though I reserve the right to ask for more paint consultations in the future. I still have the entire main floor to tackle."

"Heaven help us," Faith muttered, but she was smiling as they left the store.

Earl's cheerful "Come back soon!" followed them out.

Faith told herself the warmth in her chest was just because of the spring morning's rising temperature.

It definitely wasn't the way Ryan held the door for her, or how his hand almost but didn't quite brush hers as they walked to their trucks.

Absolutely not.

"Meet you there?" Ryan asked, pulling out his keys.

Faith nodded, already wondering what Martha's reaction would be when they walked in together. The town gossip chain was about to get a workout.

Chapter 15

Martha's eyes lit up like Christmas had come early when Faith and Ryan walked into the diner together. Faith could practically see the gossip chain activating as Martha reached for her coffee pot with suspicious efficiency.

"My favorite customers!" Martha's smile was entirely too knowing. "Let me get you a booth. The one by the window just opened up."

"Any booth is fine," Faith started to say, but Martha was already leading them to what was arguably the best seat in the house, with a view of the mountains and just enough distance from other diners for privacy.

"Coffee?" Martha didn't wait for an answer, already pouring. "The Saturday breakfast special is biscuits and gravy, but I just pulled a fresh apple pie and a fresh pecan pie from the oven."

"It's nine in the morning," Faith pointed out.

"It's never too early for pie," Ryan and Martha said in unison, then grinned at each other.

"Someone help me, there's two of them now," Faith muttered, but she was fighting a smile as she opened her menu.

"I'll give you two a minute to decide," Martha said with a wink that wasn't nearly as subtle as she probably thought it was.

An awkward silence fell as they both pretended to study menus. Faith was acutely aware that this was their first time alone together, that wasn't strictly work-related.

"So," Ryan said finally, "about that bookcase you're building..."

Faith latched onto the safe topic. "Just a simple storage project. Something to keep myself busy."

"Don't you already have plenty on your plate keeping you busy?"

"I'm not great at sitting still," Faith said, placing her menu down and locking eyes with his inquisitive stare.

"I don't mind taking a moment to just sit back and soak in the view. You know... take a little time to just do nothing and enjoy a little quiet time. These days, the swing on the farmhouse's back porch has become my favorite spot to unwind in the quiet of the evening," Ryan said with a modest smile.

"I bet life here is nothing like what you were used to in Chicago," she said.

"Not at all. Chicago moves at such a fast pace, it's like the city never sleeps. I'm finally re-learning how to slow down and just enjoy life again," he said. "I missed small-town life, actually. In Chicago, you could live next door to someone for years and never know their name. Here, everyone knows everything about everyone else."

"And that's a good thing?"

"Sometimes." Ryan thanked Martha as she delivered their breakfast plates. "Like knowing that Mrs. Jenkins always needs help carrying her groceries on Thursdays, or that Tommy at the gas station will fix a flat tire for free if you bring him a slice of Martha's coconut cream pie."

Faith watched him wave to an elderly couple across the diner. "You seem to be fitting back into Laurel Ridge pretty quickly."

"Well, I did grow up here." Ryan doctored his coffee with cream and sugar. "I forgot how much I missed it until I came back. The city has its advantages, but it can be... hollow sometimes."

"Is that why you left? The hollowness?"

Ryan was quiet for a moment, stirring his coffee. "Partly. The last big merger I worked on, I found some discrepancies in the numbers. Nothing illegal, exactly, but... the human cost was buried in footnotes. Three hundred people would lose their jobs, but the stockholders would see a two percent increase in quarterly profits."

"What did you do?"

"Tried to fight it. Suggested alternatives. Got told to 'stay in my lane' and focus on the financial projections." Ryan's usual smile had faded. "I kept thinking about my grandfather. How he always said profit without purpose was just greed wearing a nicer suit."

"Sounds like a wise man."

"He was." Ryan's expression softened. "He taught me everything important—how to measure twice and cut once, how to learn by doing and practicing, how to treat people with respect, whether they're signing your paycheck or sweeping your floors."

"Is that why you're so determined to restore part of the farmhouse yourself? To honor his memory?"

"Partly." Ryan met her eyes. "But also because some things are worth doing right, even if they're harder that way. Even if you have to learn as you go and make mistakes and possibly demolish the occasional cabinet, that turns out to be load-bearing."

"It wasn't load-bearing," Faith said automatically, then caught his teasing grin. "You're never going to let me forget that, are you?"

"Nope. It's my proudest DIY disaster so far. Though I'm sure I'll top it, eventually."

"At least you admit when you need help. That's more than I can say for some clients," Faith said.

"Speaking from experience?"

"Let's just say there's a reason we now require detailed contracts about unauthorized weekend renovations."

Their conversation flowed easily after that, moving from renovation horror stories to childhood memories of Laurel Ridge. Ryan told her about summers spent at his grandparents' farm, learning to fix fences and mend roof tiles. Faith found herself sharing stories about following her father around construction sites, and collecting wood scraps to build increasingly elaborate clubhouses.

"I still have the hammer he gave me for my sixth birthday," she admitted. "First real tool I ever owned."

"Let me guess—you slept with it under your pillow."

"Of course not." Faith felt her cheeks warm. "I kept it on the bedside table. Much more practical."

Ryan's laugh was warm and genuine. "I can just picture tiny Faith, planning home improvement projects in her sleep."

"Better than teenage Ryan watching YouTube tutorials on financial analysis."

"Hey, those tutorials got me through business school." Ryan's expression turned more serious. "Though I have to admit, working on the house feels more real than playing with numbers somehow. Making something with your hands, preserving something that matters."

Faith understood exactly what he meant. "That's why I love what I do," she found herself saying. "It's honest work. Every knot, every grain pattern, tells you exactly what you're dealing with. No hidden agendas, no nasty surprises if you know how to read it right."

"Unlike people?"

The question was gentle, but Faith felt herself tense slightly. "People are... complicated."

"They can be." Ryan's voice was careful, like he was handling something fragile. "But sometimes complications aren't always bad things."

Before Faith could respond, Martha appeared with a slice of pie and two forks. "On the house," she announced. "You two looked like you could use something sweet."

"It's still morning," she protested weakly.

"Time is an illusion," Martha declared. "Pie is eternal."

Ryan waited until she left before offering Faith a fork. "She's not wrong about the pie. Though I should warn you, I take my desserts very seriously."

"Is that a challenge?" Faith accepted the fork with a raised eyebrow. "Because I'll have you know, I once ate three pieces of Martha's cherry pie in one sitting."

"Impressive. But can you eat it while explaining the difference between mortise and tenon joints?"

"Please. I can explain proper joinery techniques in my sleep." Faith took a bite of the pecan pie, then blinked in surprise. "That is actually really good."

"Of course it is. It's Martha's." Ryan watched her take another bite. "Though I thought you said it was too early for pie?"

"Time is an illusion, remember?"

They ended up sharing not just the pie but stories about their favorite books, his college mishaps and her adventures during her youth. Faith found herself relaxing into the conversation, drawn in by Ryan's genuine interest and thoughtful questions.

"So, will I see you at church tomorrow?" he asked.

Faith glanced up, momentarily taken aback. "I'm not sure..."

"Ah, some hesitation," he remarked, his tone probing gently.

"Honestly, I'm not very consistent about going to church. I usually just attend on holidays—it makes my dad happy," she admitted.

"Faith, in case it slipped your mind, tomorrow is a holiday. It's Easter Sunday."

Caught off guard, she froze. In the whirlwind of keeping the business afloat, long workdays, and hospital visits squeezing in time with her dad, Easter had completely escaped her thoughts. "With Dad still in the hospital, it'd feel strange going without him," she murmured.

"Alright," he said with a soft smile. "No pressure. But if you change your mind, you're more than welcome to sit next to me."

Faith glanced at her watch. "I should probably get going. I want to work on my bookcase before Monica comes over tonight," she said, gently steering the subject in a new direction.

"Ah, of course," Ryan replied, signaling for the check. His expression softened further. "But I have to admit—I see what you're doing, shifting the conversation like that. I'm sorry if I overstepped or made you uncomfortable. That wasn't my intention."

"No harm done. God and I haven't exactly been on speaking terms for years."

"Mind if I ask why?"

"Let's just say when your mom walks out on you at fourteen, it makes you wonder if God was ever paying attention to begin with."

"I... I don't know what to say," he murmured. "Faith, I'm so sorry that happened to you."

"Don't be," she replied, her tone firm as she finished the last sip of her coffee. "I've already moved past it. Sympathy isn't what I need."

With that, she stood and grabbed her purse. "Thank you for your company this morning, but it's time I head home."

Ryan immediately noticed the subtle shift in her mood, the sudden coolness in her expression. He realized, too late, that he had struck a nerve unintentionally. As she reached inside her purse to retrieve her wallet, he gently placed his hand over hers and said, "Please, let me take care of this."

They stepped out together into the late morning sunlight, pausing awkwardly beside their trucks.

"This was…" Ryan's voice trailed off as he searched for the right words.

"Nice," Faith offered, immediately regretting how dull it sounded.

But the way Ryan's smile widened told her he understood perfectly. "It was. Next time, let's do dinner."

"Next time?"

"A guy can hope, can't he?"

Her lips curved into a faint smile. "We'll see," she replied before climbing into her truck.

Chapter 16

Ryan pushed the old oak door open, its familiar weight resisting just enough to evoke a whisper of nostalgia. The faint, comforting aroma of polished wood and well-loved hymnals enveloped him as he crossed the threshold. The door eased shut behind him with a soft click, sealing him in the quiet sanctuary. Sunlight poured through the intricate stained-glass windows, casting a kaleidoscope of softened reds, blues, and greens across the rows of dark wooden pews. Everything appeared smaller than he remembered, less daunting, less grand. Had the church diminished with time, or had he simply outgrown the awe he'd once felt for its simplicity?

The memory of childhood Sundays flickered in his mind, sitting in these very pews, his too-stiff suit itching at the collar as he fidgeted through Pastor Thompson's meandering sermons. His grandfather's firm hand would settle on his knee, both a quiet reprimand and a silent reminder to sit still. Back then, the church had loomed large, its walls feeling as if they had reached all the way to heaven. Now, it seemed more humble, less a towering house of worship and more a haven of quiet reflection. And yet, somehow, it still felt the same.

Ryan's childhood friend and longtime spiritual mentor, Pastor Andrew Whitman, had recently taken on the role of Laurel Ridge's pastor following the retirement of Pastor Thompson. Over the years, Andrew and Ryan had stayed in close contact, their friendship becoming a lifeline for Ryan during his college days and later, his corporate career in Chicago. Though Ryan had never quite found a church in the bustling city that felt like home, his conversations with Andrew offered comfort and guidance. Those late-night phone calls or heartfelt messages became an anchor, helping Ryan navigate struggles and find solace when he needed a place to unburden his worries and renew his faith.

Ryan's gaze traveled across the sanctuary, landing on the modest altar with its simple wooden cross. His grandparents used to have a favorite pew—fourth row back, left side. He could practically picture his grandmother there, digging through her handbag for a peppermint to keep him quiet while his grandfather mouthed along with every hymn in a voice that was as beautiful as a sunrise.

The door to Andrew's office was cracked open, and Ryan could hear rustling papers as he made his way to see his friend. It had been so long since he's seen him in person. Ryan raised a hand and knocked twice on the door frame, just loud enough to announce himself.

Andrew looked up from behind his cluttered desk, his face breaking into a wide grin. "I heard you arrived in town safely." He stood, brushing nonexistent dust off his khakis, and came around the desk to greet Ryan. "Come here, you big-city deserter."

Ryan laughed as Andrew pulled him into a firm hug, patting his back like the years hadn't mattered. "Good to see you, Pastor Whitman."

"Ah, come on now... I love the Pastor title," Andrew said, shaking his head as he released him. "But to you, I'm still just Andrew." His brown eyes danced with humor behind his reading glasses.

"Fine, Andrew it is," Ryan replied with mock deference, emphasizing the name as he gestured to the cluttered desk. "Look's like you're busy."

"Just going through some old sermons," Andrew said as he glanced at the leaning tower of files on his desk and shrugged. "So, you've been back home a few days now, what almost a week? How's it going?"

Ryan chuckled. "I've just been keeping busy with the farmhouse, trying to get things moving with the renovations."

"And how's that going?" Andrew motioned for Ryan to take a seat in one of the mismatched armchairs across from the desk. He leaned against his desk casually, arms crossed, interested but relaxed in that easy way of his.

Ryan settled into the seat, his long legs stretching out slightly. "It's... a lot. There's definitely more work than I expected, but I'm finally figuring out what I don't know, which feels like progress. I've been pacing myself—working in the kitchen — and McNeil Construction is handling the big structural stuff."

"Good company to work with. James and Faith are well known for their work in this area. I need to get out to the hospital to check on James. He's having a few health issues."

"Yeah, that's what I've heard," Ryan replied.

"So, aside from tackling farmhouse renovations, how're you settling in?"

Ryan paused, his initial answer—"fine, I guess"—catching on the tip of his tongue. Andrew was the kind of person you could give surface-level answers to, but it would only last so long before he cut straight to the heart of things. "It's been good to be back, honestly.

I'd almost forgotten how peaceful and wonderful life can be here. But it's... different."

"Different how?" Andrew prompted gently.

Ryan hesitated for a moment, then decided to speak from the heart. "Coming back home has been a true blessing. I'm not the same kid who left for college all those years ago. I've grown, I've changed. I see things through a different lens now—things I might've taken for granted before or been too busy to notice. I appreciate this place, and the people here, so much more than I ever did back then."

"Isn't it incredible how, when you look back on your life, you can see just how far we've come and how much we've grown?"

"It really is. It's been great reconnecting with people I hadn't seen in years. With some, it feels like no time has passed at all—like I never even left."

Andrew nodded, his face creasing in understanding. "How's your parents?"

Ryan let out a dry laugh. "They're doing good. Still the same Thomas and Meg I'm sure you remember from way back when. They think I'm crazy for leaving behind a partnership track and a seven-figure salary to fix up the farmhouse. They've called a few times, surface-level conversations about nothing, just to make sure I still have a pulse. But support? Encouragement? Those aren't in their wheelhouse."

Andrew studied him for a long moment. "That has to be tough."

Ryan shifted in his seat, his hands clasped loosely in his lap. "It is. And I don't hold it against them... not entirely. They just don't know how to connect. I've made peace with that—or at least I'm trying. But there are times when it stings, you know? I'll send them pictures of the progress or share plans, hoping for a reaction, and all I get is, 'Looks like a lot of work' or something equally vague."

Andrew leaned back against the desk, his expression thoughtful. "You know, Ryan, there's a verse in Proverbs that always helps me when I'm wrestling with unmet expectations. 'Commit your work to the Lord, and your plans will be established.' It's not about people approving or understanding; it's about surrendering the parts we can't control to God's care. That's what frees us to focus on the pieces we can control."

Ryan looked up at him, a small smile forming. "I guess that's easier to preach than practice, huh?"

"Oh, absolutely," Andrew said with an easy laugh. "But it changes how you approach things. When you let go of trying to change others and focus on what God's asking you to do, the weights shift a little. Let God handle the rebuilding in His timing."

Ryan nodded slowly, mulling over the thought. "Patience, I believe, is the answer to many things in life."

"Well... that and a good cup of coffee," Andrew said with a small grin, lifting his mug slightly as if to toast the sentiment. "But on a more serious note, have you thought about inviting your parents to visit? Let them see this new life you're building for yourself. It might help bridge some of the distance."

Ryan's brow furrowed thoughtfully. "You know, that's an idea I hadn't really considered. Though I seriously doubt they would come."

Andrew leaned back, his tone shifting to something more reflective. "The relationship between parents and their adult children can be... well, let's call it a delicate dance. They want so much for you, and when you take a path that doesn't match their expectations, it can throw them completely off balance. For people like your parents, who are so focused and goal-oriented, it's not always easy for them to adapt to a new paradigm."

"You mean because they're stuck in their straight-line way of thinking?" Ryan asked, a trace of self-awareness coloring his voice.

Andrew nodded. "Exactly. They're career-driven, pragmatic, and a little emotionally stilted, if I'm being honest. It doesn't mean they don't care; it just means they're not always great at showing it—or at pivoting when life doesn't unfold the way they envisioned. I think they need a nudge... or maybe several nudges."

Ryan let out a faint chuckle, more out of irony than humor. "So you're saying I might have to reach out repeatedly before it even begins to sink in?"

"Exactly," Andrew said, his voice steady and warm. "Consistency could be what they need—seeing the changes in you firsthand, over time. They may not understand the choices you've made yet, but don't underestimate the power of showing them who you're becoming. That speaks louder than anything you could say."

"I've spent so much of my life wondering why God gave me the parents I have," Ryan said, his voice tinged with quiet reflection. "I've questioned why they are the way they are—why they could never be the kind of parents who are loving, supportive, and truly involved. Don't get me wrong, I know they love me... in their own distant, complicated way. But feeling that love? That's always been rare."

Andrew leaned forward slightly, resting his hands on his knees, his gaze steady and compassionate. "Ryan, have you ever thought that maybe God doesn't just give us relationships to fulfill us, but also to shape us? Parents, friendships, even romantic relationships, they all have a way of sanding off our rough edges, sometimes painfully, but always with a purpose. Your parents' distance has pushed you to value connection in a way they never could. Their shortcomings gave you the resolve to become a different kind of man."

"'Strength forged in scarcity,',' Ryan said. "Those are the words my grandpa used to say to me. I agree with everything you've said. I've made it a point in my life to be a better man and, hopefully, someday a good father."

Andrew nodded, his smile encouraging. "Well, just remember relationships, especially the messy ones, take time to rebuild. Don't expect it all to change overnight—just focus on the steps you can take and let God handle the rest."

Ryan exhaled a quiet laugh. "You know, you make this sound a lot easier than it feels."

Andrew's grin crinkled the corners of his eyes. "That's my job—it's in the fine print of the 'Pastor Whitman Handbook.'" He paused for a moment, growing quiet. "But seriously, Ryan, you're not walking this road alone. Whether it's bridging the gap with your parents or navigating life back in Laurel Ridge, you've got people here who care about you, and a God who's never stopped walking beside you."

"And for that, I'm thankful," Ryan said, his voice soft but sincere.

"So, how about Easter service tomorrow? I assume you'll grace us with your presence?"

Ryan nodded, an easy smile finding its way back to his face. "I'll be there. Wouldn't miss it."

Andrew gave a satisfied nod. "Good... good. I look forward to having you here with us."

"You remember where I live now, right? Come by the farmhouse sometime and see how it's coming along," Ryan said, his tone light but inviting. "There's already a lot of progress to show."

"I might just take you up on that," Andrew replied thoughtfully. "Honestly, it's been a while since I've had an excuse to pick up a hammer. It'd be nice to step away and get my hands dirty for a change."

"Well, consider this your open invitation," Ryan said with a grin. "There's no shortage of work waiting to be tackled."

As Andrew's contagious laugh echoed softly in the room, Ryan felt a wave of comfort settle over him. Laurel Ridge might have been smaller, slower, and less polished than the life he'd left behind in Chicago, but here, in this quiet church office surrounded by sermon notes and the warmth of an old friendship, there was something he hadn't realized he craved: belonging.

The two men parted with a handshake and a few light-hearted words, their farewells as warm and easy as the morning itself. Ryan lingered on the church's wide front steps, hands resting in his pockets as the door clicked shut behind him. The crisp, cool air carried the faint scent of blooming dogwood and freshly turned soil, mingling with the distant, comforting hum of small-town life. Before him, the Appalachian mountains unfurled like a painter's masterpiece, their slopes brushed with the tender green of early spring. The sunlight caught on their ridges, casting soft shadows that played across the landscape. The sky, a delicate eggshell blue, stretched endlessly overhead, unmarred by clouds, giving the world an unspoken promise of tranquility.

Ryan tilted his head toward the heavens, his voice soft but resolute. "Lord, thank You for this life, for the blessings I often overlook. Thank You for the friends who ground me and remind me of what truly matters. Thank You for shaping me through the people You've placed in my life, even the challenges they bring. Guide me, Father, as I walk this path. Show me how to fulfill the purpose You've set before me with faith and grace."

Chapter 17

Monica burst through Faith's apartment door with the confidence of someone who'd done it a million times before, deftly juggling a pizza box and a two liter bottle of pop.

"I'm here, and let me tell you, those stairs are going to be the death of me," she announced, closing the door with her foot for emphasis. "But, I made it. I come bearing carbs and conversation!"

Faith looked up from where she sat on the couch, and Monica's jovial entrance slowed. Her friend wasn't working on anything—no tools in hand, no project spread out around her. Just sitting there, looking pensive, in a way that set off all of Monica's best-friend warning bells.

"Okay, what's wrong?" Monica set the pizza and pop on the coffee table. "And don't say nothing."

Faith managed a weak smile. "Can't a person just sit and think?"

"You? Sit still?" Monica headed to the kitchen for glasses and plates. "The last time you sat still and looked dazed, your dad had been admitted to the hospital. So spill."

"It's not Dad." Faith ran a hand through her hair, which was still slightly damp from a shower. "He's actually doing a little better. Dr. Benson says his numbers are improving."

"Good. Then this must be about your breakfast with Ryan."

Faith's head snapped up. "How did you—"

"I saw both your trucks outside the diner this morning." Monica returned with glasses and plates, settling onto the couch. "And before you say it wasn't a date, I know. But something happened, didn't it?"

Faith was quiet for a moment. "Nothing happened. That's the weird part. We just... talked. For two hours."

"About?"

"Everything. Nothing. Paint samples and childhood memories and why he left Chicago." Faith took a long sip of her drink that Monica had poured for her. "Did you know his grandfather taught him basic carpentry? That's why he's so determined to do some of the work himself."

"Interesting." Monica's tone was carefully neutral as she opened the pizza box. "But that's not what's bothering you."

"No." Faith stared into her glass. "What's bothering me is how easy it was. How natural it felt, just sitting there talking about nothing important."

"And heaven forbid you actually enjoy someone's company," Monica teased gently.

"You know, it's not that simple."

"Why not?" Monica settled back with her pizza. "And before you start listing all your very practical reasons, let me tell you about my coffee date yesterday. Mr. 'My Ex-Wife Would Have Hated This Coffee Shop' spent forty-five minutes explaining why his divorce wasn't his fault, then asked if I wanted to see pictures of their wedding."

Faith winced. "Please tell me you didn't."

"Oh, I did. All thirty-eight of them." Monica's dramatic eye roll got a genuine laugh from Faith. "And do you know what I thought the whole time? That at thirty-two, I'm too old for this nonsense. I want someone who's actually present, who sees me as a person and not just a replacement for whatever they think they're missing."

"And you think Ryan sees me?" Faith's voice was quiet.

"I think he sees you better than most." Monica studied her friend. "And I think that terrifies you."

Faith picked at her pizza. "What if I'm not ready to be seen?"

The vulnerability in her voice made Monica's heart ache. "Because of your mom?" she said bluntly.

"Monica—"

"No, hear me out." Monica set down her plate. "You were fourteen when she left. Old enough to understand, but young enough that it shaped everything about how you see relationships. And I get it—watching someone walk away from you without looking back, especially a mother? That leaves scars, honey. That hurts. That is something that should never happen to anyone. Yet, it does..."

"I don't want to talk about her."

"I know you don't. But honey, she's there in everything you do, every relationship you don't let happen. Because you allow her leaving to be central and always present." Monica's voice was gentle but firm. "You've turned not needing anyone into an art form."

"Because needing people is dangerous," Faith said. "They leave. They always leave."

"I haven't."

Faith's smile was watery. "You're different."

"Your dad hasn't."

"That's different too. You and dad are both good human beings," Faith said.

"Has Ryan done anything to make you think otherwise?" Monica's voice was calm but firm as she waited for Faith to look her in the eye. "Here's what I see when I look at him: a man who could've hired anyone in the county but chose us. Someone who's not just fixing up a house, but rebuilding his life. I see a kind, genuine person, the kind who's interesting and fun to be around. And honestly, Faith, I think he came into your life for a reason."

"That's what scares me." Faith set down her untouched pizza.

"Romans 8:28—'And we know that in all things God works for the good of those who love him, who have been called according to his purpose.'"

Faith's expression closed slightly. "You know how I feel about that."

"I know you've been angry at God since your mom left. That was eighteen years ago. I'm not saying you should get over or forget what your mother did, but maybe it's time to start moving forward in life. Set what happened to you aside a little and start moving in a good direction. Faith, what if Ryan is part of God's purpose? What if Ryan showing up now, when you're dealing with your dad's health and the business pressure—what if that's not a complication but a provision?"

"I stopped believing in that kind of thing a long time ago."

"No, you stopped letting yourself hope for it. There's a difference." Monica reached for her friend's hand. "Not everyone leaves, Faith. Some people show up exactly when they're meant to and stay exactly as long as they're needed."

"And what if Ryan's not one of those people?"

"What if he is?" Monica squeezed her hand. "What if this is your chance to find out?"

Faith pulled her hand away. "It's not that simple. It just can't be."

"Nothing worth having ever is. But you can't keep using your mother or the business as an excuse not to live your life. Your dad wouldn't want that. I don't want that."

"I know." Faith's voice was barely audible. "But from the moment I met Ryan, something felt different. And not just attraction, though..." She flushed slightly. "That's definitely there. But it's more than that. Like something shifted, and now everything I thought I knew about my life feels... off-balance."

"Maybe that's not a bad thing." Monica's smile was understanding. "Sometimes we need to lose our balance a little to find our feet again."

"I'm just not cut out for all this lovey-dovey stuff. Pretty sure God skipped me when he was handing out that particular skill set."

"Oh, stop it, Faith. You're more loving and kind than you give yourself credit for. You share so much of that goodness every single day—you just don't even see it."

Faith's phone buzzed, and Monica didn't miss the way her friend's expression softened when she saw the screen.

"Your face just did a thing."

"My face did not do a thing."

"It absolutely did." Monica grinned. "A soft, mushy, completely non-professional thing. Let me guess—Ryan?"

Faith set her phone down without responding, but her lips curved slightly. "Eat your pizza."

"Not until you tell me what he said."

"He just..." Faith's cheeks colored. "He asked if I wanted to meet him after church tomorrow for lunch. To thank me for helping with the paint samples."

"And?"

"And nothing."

Monica reached over and grabbed Faith's phone, quickly typing before Faith could stop her. "There. Now you have."

"Monica!" Faith snatched her phone back, reading with horror.

"What?" Monica's grin was unrepentant.

Faith groaned. "I hate you right now."

"You love me. And you'll thank me tomorrow when you're having lunch with a man who actually wants to spend time with you," Monica said. "So, church? It's Easter Sunday. Do you want to come with me and then meet Ryan for lunch afterward?"

"No, Monica."

"Faith, you should come. You know it would make your dad happy, and besides, I want you to be there," Monica said, her voice soft but insistent.

Faith sighed, glancing at her friend. "I was planning to visit Dad at the hospital tomorrow," she started, her tone guarded. Then, after a moment's hesitation, she added, "But... I'll think about it."

Faith's phone buzzed again. She peeked at it, then quickly looked away, but not before Monica caught her smile.

"Your face did another thing."

"Oh, hush."

Monica complied, watching her friend try and fail to suppress her smile as she typed a response.

Chapter 18

Monica burst into Faith's apartment like a tornado... again, though this time dressed in a floral print dress ready for church.

"Rise and shine, sleeping beauty. Get up, get dressed, and grab your Bible... if you even know where it is. You're coming to church with me."

Faith groaned from the couch, where she'd been lounging in sweats, halfheartedly scrolling through her phone. She shot Monica a glare that had no real bite. "You know, normal people knock."

"And you'd let me in? Please." Monica set her tote and mug on the counter. "This is a 'drag-you-to-what's-good-for-you' emergency. No time for formalities."

"You know," Faith called back, "this is exactly why I'm going to start locking my door."

"Please. I'd just use my emergency key."

Faith sat up, running a hand through her sleep-mussed hair. "The key I gave you for actual emergencies?"

"This is an emergency. It's Easter Sunday, and my best friend is in danger of spending it alone with power tools." Monica headed straight for Faith's closet. "Now, are you going to pick out something appropriate to wear, or should I?"

"I was already planning to go," Faith admitted quietly.

Monica stopped mid-rummage through Faith's clothes. "Wait, what?"

"Don't make it a thing." Faith got up from the couch and, pushing past her friend, to grab the dress she'd laid out the night before. "I just... thought it might be nice. For Dad."

Monica's expression softened. "Just for your dad?"

"And maybe..." Faith busied herself gathering shoes and accessories. "Maybe because someone reminded me that not everyone leaves."

"Honey." Monica's voice wobbled slightly. "Now I'm going to cry and ruin my mascara."

"Don't you dare. I'm not explaining to your mother why you showed up to Easter service looking like a raccoon." Faith disappeared into the bathroom to change.

Twenty minutes later, they pulled into the church parking lot. Faith's stomach tightened as she took in the familiar white clapboard building with its tall steeple. How many Easters had she spent here as a child, wearing scratchy dresses and patent leather shoes, holding her father's hand during hymns? And later in life, on holidays, beside her father.

Now, standing at the foot of the wide wooden steps, she hesitated.

"You okay?" Monica asked.

Faith nodded. "Yeah."

"Hey." Monica looped her arm through Faith's and gave a little tug. "It's just a building. The important thing is what you get out of it. And let's be honest, you could use a spiritual tune-up."

"Subtle, as always." But the corner of Faith's mouth twitched upward, and she let Monica guide her inside.

The sanctuary was already buzzing with quiet conversation as people found their seats. Faith scanned the room instinctively, her eyes landing on a familiar figure standing near the far aisle.

Ryan.

Monica spotted him at the same time and wasted no time waving enthusiastically. Faith, torn between annoyance and nerves, managed a small, forced wave of her own. Ryan's face lit up when he saw them. He excused himself from Pastor Andrew, who he'd been speaking with, and made his way toward them, his easy, confident stride making Faith suddenly self-conscious.

"Good morning, ladies," he greeted with a broad smile that somehow felt personal when his gaze lingered on Faith. "Happy Easter."

"Happy Easter, Ryan," Monica chirped, clearly enjoying herself. "We're going to grab a pew over there. Care to join us?"

"I'd love to," Ryan said, his eyes still on Faith. If he noticed the slight pink creeping into her cheeks, he didn't comment.

Monica led the way, slipping into the pew first. Faith followed reluctantly, leaving Ryan to slide in beside her.

"You okay?" Ryan asked.

"Fine." Faith smoothed her dress, buying time. "Just... been a while."

"God doesn't mind gaps in attendance." His tone held no judgment, just quiet understanding. "He's pretty good at welcoming people home."

The sanctuary began quieting as Pastor Whitman stepped up to the pulpit, his warm expression bringing an immediate sense of calm to the room.

"Good morning, and welcome," the pastor began, his voice steady and kind. "Today, we gather to celebrate the greatest story ever told—the story of hope, of redemption, and of a love that conquers all." His words carried an earnestness that had Faith shifting slightly in her seat, uneasy but not entirely closed off.

Ryan sat beside her, his posture relaxed but attentive. She caught herself glancing at him more than once, curious about his serene focus. How could he sit here so at ease, so unquestioningly sure of... all of this?

The sermon was thoughtfully delivered, not too heavy-handed, focusing on themes of grace and renewal. Faith found herself listening, despite herself. She wouldn't call it conviction exactly, but something about Pastor Whitman's words stirred a feeling she couldn't quite name—like a door cracked open just enough to let in a sliver of light.

After the service, Pastor Whitman invited everyone to gather outside for the annual Easter Egg Hunt, a tradition Faith remembered well. She had dismissed it as silly back when she was a teenager, but now, as an adult, watching the kids dart around with their baskets and uncontainable glee, she felt an unexpected fondness for it.

"This is chaos, but the kids are fun to watch," she said as she stood with Monica and Ryan near the edge of the field. Parents hollered encouragement while toddlers stumbled after glittery eggs.

"Organized chaos," Ryan corrected. "That's what makes it fun."

Monica grinned. "You're both wrong. This is prime entertainment. Look, Mrs. Hensley is practically crawling under that picnic table for her grandson."

Faith couldn't help but laugh. "Why do I feel like we should offer backup?"

"Because you're a fixer," Ryan said without missing a beat. "If these eggs were construction projects, you'd already have a plan of attack."

She shot him a look. "Oh, come on... I would not."

"You two behave," Monica teased as she walked away to join her parents.

Faith suddenly felt exposed, standing next to Ryan without the buffer of Monica's constant banter.

"Did you enjoy the service?" he asked, his tone quiet, almost hesitant.

"Yeah," she said. "I actually did."

Ryan didn't press her, just nodded thoughtfully. "I'm glad you came."

Faith glanced at him, unsure how to respond. Before she could overthink it, he asked, "Still up for lunch?"

"Sure. I skipped breakfast, so I'm definitely hungry."

"Well, there's a minor problem. When I invited you, I didn't stop to think about it being Easter Sunday. All the restaurants in town are closed."

"Right. I didn't stop to think about that, either." Faith tried to ignore the slight disappointment in her chest. "Another time, maybe."

"Or..." Ryan looked almost nervous. "I might have packed a picnic. Nothing fancy, just some sandwiches and stuff."

"A picnic?" She arched an eyebrow. "You packed a picnic lunch?"

"Is that weird? It's weird, isn't it?" Ryan ran a hand through his hair. "I just thought... but if you'd rather not—"

"No, it's...thoughtful," Faith said. "This day is just turning out to be full of surprises."

Ryan's smile widened, his hazel eyes crinkling in a way that made her stomach flip. "Surprises can be good sometimes."

She didn't respond right away; her gaze lingering on him longer than she intended. Something about the way he stood there, so genuine, so steady—it was unnerving in the best and worst ways. Around them, children shouted triumphantly over found eggs, parents chatted in small groups, and the spring breeze carried the scent of blooming dogwoods. It felt... right, somehow. Like something clicking into place that she hadn't known was misaligned.

"Alright," she said finally. "Let's see what you've got, picnic master."

Ryan's chuckle was low and warm as he gestured toward the parking lot. "After you."

As they walked toward his truck to retrieve the picnic supplies, Faith felt that familiar tug-of-war inside her chest—the life she'd carefully constructed versus this pull toward something more. Something that scared her even as it drew her in.

But watching Ryan navigate through the crowd, stopping to help a small boy retrieve an egg from a bush, Faith wondered if maybe Monica was right. Maybe some people showed up exactly when they were meant to. Maybe some people were worth the risk of getting to know.

Maybe some renovations started with the heart.

Chapter 19

Ryan opened the passenger side door of his truck with an easy smile, stepping aside to let Faith climb in. She raised an eyebrow at him, already suspicious.

"You know," she said, crossing her arms as she lingered near the open door, "there's a perfectly good pavilion behind the church. Flat ground, fresh air... not to mention it's only a few hundred yards that way." She jerked her head toward the back of the church, where the pavilion was tucked neatly against the backdrop of the mountains.

Ryan's grin widened. "Well, I have a surprise."

Faith tilted her head, skeptical. "A surprise?"

He stepped back and gestured toward the inside of the truck with exaggerated chivalry. "Come on. Humor me."

With an exasperated sigh and a shake of her head, Faith climbed into the truck. "This better not involve anything weird. I don't do weird, Ryan."

He leaned in slightly as he closed her door, his hazel eyes sparkling with mischief. "Noted."

Faith could only roll her eyes as she watched him stride around the front of the truck. Though she tried—and failed—not to notice the easy way he carried himself, or the way he tossed her a quick grin before climbing into the driver's seat.

When he settled in beside her, she buckled in and gave him an expectant look. "Okay, where are we going?"

Ryan started the engine but didn't answer, pulling out of the parking lot as smoothly as if he were stalling for time.

"Ryan?"

He chuckled, glancing her way. "Alright, alright. Full disclosure—it wasn't all my idea."

"Let me guess. Monica had something to do with this," Faith said, her eyes narrowing in mock suspicion.

"You'd be correct." Ryan's grin widened as he turned onto the winding road that led out of Laurel Ridge. "She swung by last night after she left your place. Said she had an idea to make today a little more special. And, well..." He shrugged as though it were the most natural thing in the world. "I thought she was onto something."

"And what exactly are we doing?" Faith's tone was cautious, but curious.

Ryan glanced over his shoulder toward the back seat, where the picnic basket sat wedged securely. "We're still having a picnic," he said, his eyes flicking back to hers with a teasing smile. "Just... not in the traditional way."

Faith frowned, clearly unimpressed by his cryptic response. "Should I be worried?"

He laughed, the sound warm and genuine, cutting through her skepticism like sunshine. "No. Absolutely not. But I couldn't have Easter lunch with you and not include your dad. So... we're going to the hospital to have a picnic with him."

For a moment, silence filled the cab. Faith blinked, her lips parting as if to speak, but no words came. Of all the things she might have guessed, this wasn't one of them. She felt the sting of tears welling up, an unfamiliar sensation she fought to suppress with all her might.

"You're serious," she finally said, her voice quieter than before. She looked at him, her eyes shimmering with the weight of unshed tears, teetering on the edge of breaking free.

Ryan nodded, still focused on the road. "It's Easter. It felt right. Figured he could use a little cheer, and you could use some time with him."

Faith stared down at her hands, her fingers twisting together in a restless dance. For someone who always seemed to have the right tools—even the right words—this moment rendered her defenseless. The ache blooming in her chest was unfamiliar and sharp, leaving her unmoored. Everything in her life felt tilted, as if the foundation she'd depended on had shifted again without warning, leaving her struggling to find her footing.

"You did this for my dad?" she asked softly, then hesitated. "For me?"

"Of course I did," Ryan said, as he glanced her way. "Oh, no... I didn't mean to upset you," he added quickly, noticing the shimmer in her eyes. His voice softened further, edged with genuine concern. "Please don't cry. That wasn't my intention at all. I just..." He hesitated, searching for the right words, his hand hovering as if he wasn't sure whether to reach for hers. "I just wanted you to enjoy the day."

She let out a shaky laugh, her voice tinged with emotion. "I swear, I'm not usually the kind of person who cries at everything—really, I'm not. But this, Ryan..." Her hand moved to her chest as her voice softened. "This got me. Right here."

He reached over and took her hand, his touch so effortless it felt as though it had always been meant to happen. She stared down at their intertwined fingers, her voice soft and uncertain. "I'm not good at this, Ryan."

He turned to look at her, his hazel eyes calm and steady. "Good at what?" he asked gently, giving her hand a reassuring squeeze.

"I haven't really dated much," she admitted, her voice low and hesitant. "Honestly, I'm not even sure I know how to do this."

He turned to her with a reassuring smile. "There's nothing you have to do," he said gently. "Dating isn't about following a set of rules—it's just about being yourself, trusting your instincts, and seeing where it takes you. I think that's what makes this... us... work. It feels natural, doesn't it? Like we're finding our rhythm without even trying."

She glanced out the window, unsure how to respond to that, so naturally, she settled on sarcasm. "I hope you didn't pack anything too unhealthy. The nurses are going to have a field day if you bring him fried chicken and chocolate cake."

"Chocolate cake makes everything better," Ryan deadpanned, a grin tugging at his lips.

"Except blood sugar levels," Faith quipped.

"Well, I didn't pack any fried chicken or chocolate cake," he admitted. "But... there might be cookies."

"You're bringing cookies to a cardiac ward."

"Just a few! For morale," Ryan said, clearly fighting back a laugh.

Faith shook her head, pressing a hand to her temple as if trying to process this absurd, wonderful man sitting beside her. "You're impossible."

"And yet, here we are," he shot back with a wink.

As the narrow mountain roads stretched ahead of them, Faith leaned back in her seat, the initial wave of shock giving way to something softer. Something harder to name. It was a quiet sort of gratitude wrapped in disbelief, peppered with a cautious hope she had never felt.

She glanced sideways at him, watching as his hand flexed on the steering wheel, steady and sure, his other still held onto hers. He hadn't moved mountains or performed miracles; he'd done something simple, thoughtful, and deeply kind. The kind of thing she'd stopped believing people did without ulterior motives.

"Well," she muttered, looking out the window to hide the emotions creeping into her eyes again, "this is officially the weirdest Easter I've ever had."

Ryan's chuckle filled the cab, low and warm. "Let's see if we can make it the best, too."

***

By the time they arrived at the hospital parking lot, Faith's nerves had mostly evened out, though a faint flutter still lingered under the surface. She hesitated for a moment, watching Ryan as he stepped out and rounded the truck to open her door. There was something disarming about his easy, unhurried movements—steady and confident in a way that left her feeling soft, almost delicate... feminine.

"Do you need help with that?" she asked as he tucked a thermos under his arm and hefted the basket in his other hand.

"Absolutely not." He gave her a crooked grin. "Let me be the pack mule for one day."

Faith raised an eyebrow. "What, do you think chivalry is still alive or something?"

Ryan pretended to consider her question. "I'd like to think it's at least on life support."

She rolled her eyes, but a soft laugh escaped before she could stop it.

Inside the hospital, Faith led the way to James's room, her heels clicking lightly against the linoleum while Ryan walked beside her. She found herself stealing glances at him, as if waiting for the dream to dissolve. Moments like this didn't happen to her—not the easy companionship, not the fireworks that seemed to linger in the air between them. She was used to navigating life on her own, with her dad as the lone exception. And years spent working in a male-dominated field had left her feeling out of place among other women, as though the softer, more nurturing traits had somehow passed her by. Life had sharpened her edges, toughened her demeanor, and made her question whether she still carried any of the tenderness she saw so effortlessly in the few women who drifted in and out of her world.

When they reached the door to room 412, Faith paused, glancing back at him. "He's probably expecting a boring lunch tray with green Jell-O. This might be a shock to his system."

Ryan arched a brow, a playful glint in his hazel eyes. "Are you saying I should dial back the charm?"

Faith hesitated, then smirked. "Not at all. Honestly, I kind of like it. Besides," she added, her tone light but teasing, "I think my dad might find all of this... entertaining."

Ryan's grin widened, warm and easy, as she opened the door.

Chapter 20

"Happy Easter, Dad," Faith said, her voice steady as she stepped inside to see her dad sitting upright in bed, flipping through an old issue of Field & Stream.

James looked up, his face lighting with surprise. "Well, I'll be."

He looked between his daughter and the man standing beside her, one brow arched in curiosity. Faith could see the questions swirling in his eyes, the same mix of confusion and intrigue she had wrestled with more than once today.

Faith grinned, moving to hug him gently. "We brought lunch."

"We?" James looked past her, towards Ryan. His mouth twitched with amusement. "This must be Ryan. You're a bit taller than I remember."

Ryan chuckled, unfazed. He set the picnic basket down, then extended his hand toward James, his smile confident and warm. "It's good to officially meet you again, Mr. McNeil," he said, his tone steady and genuine.

"It's good to see you again, too. It's been quite a few years. You bring coffee? The real stuff and not this black sludge they serve in this place?"

"No hospital coffee, sir," Ryan promised, holding up a thermos.

"Well, I guess you're a good man then," James teased, his gruff tone undercut by the warmth in his smile.

Faith sat in the chair beside the bed, shaking her head as Ryan began unpacking the basket onto James's rolling tray table. Thick hoagie rolls piled high with an assortment of deli meats and crisp toppings, vibrant fresh fruit cups neatly arranged in colorful bursts, and yes—cookies, soft and inviting—emerged one by one from the basket. Along with neatly folded napkins and a selection of condiments.

"Did you do all this yourself?" Faith asked.

Ryan's grin was unrepentant. "Guilty as charged."

Faith looked at her dad, who was regarding her with a mix of surprise and approval.

"You're telling me you didn't put all this together, Faith?" he asked, gesturing at the spread before him.

She shook her head, smiling. "Not even a little, Dad," she said, motioning toward Ryan. "This was all his doing."

"Either these meds they have me on are stronger than I realized, or the world's taken a turn for the downright peculiar," he said, shaking his head with a bemused smile. "But I'm not going to complain one bit. Now, young man, what kind of sandwich is this?"

Ryan chuckled as he unwrapped a sandwich and handed it to him. "These are Italian hoagie subs—a staple I learned to appreciate back in my Chicago days." He placed a container of giardiniera nearby, alongside two small styrofoam cups holding olive oil and vinegar.

James inspected the sandwich with interest before nodding in approval. "Well now, this looks a whole lot better than the cardboard they call food around here."

"I brought along some giardiniera—Italian pickled vegetables—and a little something extra," Ryan said, gesturing toward the two small containers. "This is olive oil and vinegar," he explained, handing James a plastic spoon. "Try drizzling a bit on your sandwich—it'll take it up a notch."

James followed Ryan's instructions, carefully drizzling a bit of the oil and vinegar over the sandwich before folding it back together. He took a deliberate bite, his jaw working steadily as he chewed. His expression shifted slowly, a thoughtful furrow of his brow giving way to an approving nod as he swallowed.

"Well now," James said, his voice carrying a note of genuine surprise. "This is downright impressive. I might have to start asking you for recipes."

Ryan chuckled, clearly pleased. "Glad it passes muster. The real credit goes to a Chicago deli I used to frequent—I just stole their secrets."

Faith sat back in her chair, her gaze shifting between her father and Ryan. For once, she found herself at a loss for words. There was something disarming about the easy camaraderie between the two men, something she hadn't expected but couldn't seem to look away from. Her father, usually reserved and stoic with most people, was leaning into the kind of lighthearted banter that felt... unfamiliar, yet oddly comforting and charming. And Ryan—well, Ryan seemed to belong in the moment, like he'd been part of their lives forever.

Faith cleared her throat, trying to shake the strange warmth blossoming in her chest. "Dad, if I'd known all it took to lighten your mood was a good sandwich, I would've done this years ago."

"Nice try, kid," James replied, shooting her a playful but pointed look.

Faith tilted her head, curiosity evident in her hazel eyes as she glanced toward Ryan. "Where did you get all of this? I know for a fact that our little grocery store in Laurel Ridge doesn't carry half this stuff."

Ryan's lips curved into a small, boyish grin as he leaned back slightly, resting one hand on the edge of the table. "Well, I decided to do a little exploring yesterday. I ended up driving over to Summersville. They've got a huge grocery store there, better selection than I expected. Picked up a few odds and ends while I was there."

Her brow arched ever so slightly. "You drove all the way to Summersville?"

He shrugged, his tone casual but with an undercurrent of warmth. "I needed the drive. Clears my head, and I was in the mood to explore. Plus, it felt good to stock up on a few things—and clearly, it wasn't a wasted trip."

James, mid-bite, chimed in with a teasing grin. "It's clear you're trying to win points over here, son. And I have to say, you're doing a pretty fine job of it."

Ryan chuckled, rubbing the back of his neck, while Faith, despite herself, felt her lips twitch into a smile.

James glanced between his daughter and Ryan, a sly smile forming at the corners of his lips. "Well, don't just stand there like statues," he said, motioning to the food spread across the tray table. "Grab a sandwich and sit down. A man shouldn't have to eat alone, especially on Easter."

Faith hesitated, her gaze flickering to Ryan, who was already reaching for a sandwich. His easy, casual movements seemed to put James at ease, but the flutter in her stomach wouldn't settle. She shook her head and reached for a paper plate, handing it to Ryan before grabbing one for herself.

Ryan passed her a sandwich, their fingers brushing briefly. It was nothing—just an accidental touch—but it sent an unexpected warmth zipping through her. She immediately busied herself unwrapping the sandwich, hoping no one noticed the flush creeping into her cheeks.

"Well, this is a first," James said, his tone half-teasing as he picked up his sandwich again. "Can't remember ever having a good meal in a hospital."

"I should have snuck some better food in for you," she said.

"You know, Faith," James said, his voice dipping into that softer, dad-wisdom tone she'd heard a thousand times before, "it's not just about the food, now that I think about it. It's about who as well. And right now, I can't think of better company to have a meal with."

That simple statement wrapped itself around Faith's heart. She swallowed hard and glanced at Ryan. "Thank you for this."

"You're welcome Faith."

When the sandwiches were gone, Ryan reached for the cookies, unwrapping them with a flourish. "Alright, who's up for a little dessert?"

"I don't know," Faith teased, leaning back in her chair with a mock-serious expression. "You brought cookies to a cardiac unit. Shouldn't we clear that with a nurse first?"

"Listen," Ryan said, his voice dropping into a stage whisper as he handed James a cookie. "It's one cookie. And technically, it's fruit-based." He continued as he broke a cookie in half, revealing chunks of dried cranberries inside. "See? Practically health food."

James chuckled, taking the cookie and inspecting it like a man appraising gold. "Well, here's to health food..."

Faith rolled her eyes, but reached for a cookie of her own. "You're impossible. Both of you."

Ryan only grinned, unrepentant.

It felt good to see her dad's spirits lifted, the lines of fatigue on his face softening ever so slightly. And it felt... nice having Ryan there, his easy demeanor an anchor in a day that seemed to have caught her off balance from the very beginning.

When James finally leaned back with a satisfied sigh, Ryan began tidying up the remnants of their lunch. Faith stood to help, but he waved her off. "Sit," he said with a smile. "I've got this."

James watched Ryan as he efficiently cleaned up the lunch mess, his movements unhurried but purposeful. As Ryan tucked the empty containers back into the picnic basket, he straightened and offered James and Faith a warm smile.

"I'll take this down to the truck," he said, hefting the basket easily. "Give you two some time to catch up." His tone was casual, but the thoughtfulness in his words was evident.

With a slight nod to Faith and a polite tip of his chin toward James, Ryan made his way out of the room.

"He seems like a good man," James said.

Faith's breath hitched slightly, her eyes darting to her dad's face. His expression was unreadable, but the way he held her gaze felt like he was weighing something in his mind.

"Yeah. I believe he is."

"You've been smiling almost the whole time you've been here," James said.

"Have I?"

James tilted his head, narrowing his eyes at her in that way only he could. "Don't act so surprised, kid. I might be stuck in this bed for now, but I'm not blind. Smiling looks good on you."

"Maybe it's just the sunshine," she hedged, motioning toward the window where warm spring light filtered in. "It's hard not to smile when the world finally thaws out after a long winter."

"Nice try."

"What?" Faith felt her cheeks burn.

James chuckled. "Honey, I've been on this earth far longer than you. I know the look of a man who's trying, and I mean really trying, to make an impression. And whether you want to admit it to me or not, I'd wager you like the way he looks doing it."

Faith grinned and nodded her head. "Yeah, dad, I think I do."

Chapter 21

"Thank you," Faith said, glancing over at Ryan as he eased the truck onto the winding country road. "I really mean it, Ryan. Thank you for today. For everything. For driving me to the hospital, for bringing lunch—" she exhaled a quiet laugh under her breath—"for showing my dad that sandwiches can go beyond peanut butter and jelly."

Ryan chuckled, gripping the steering wheel. "I think your dad's exact words were 'downright impressive.' Though I might've noticed him eyeing the cookies as if they came straight from Heaven's bakery."

"They might as well have," Faith teased, leaning her elbow against the window's edge, her gaze flicking toward the side mirror to see the hospital shrinking in the distance. "But seriously... you made today so special for my dad. For me. Nobody's ever gone out of their way like that for me before."

"Well," he said, his voice low and sincere, "It was good to see you smile, and that makes it worth it to me."

She tucked a loose strand of hair behind her ear and glanced at him, her voice soft but heartfelt. "Ryan, I don't think I'll ever forget what you did today. Seeing my dad smile like that... It meant everything. I could tell we truly made his day."

"I'm glad," Ryan said, his smile both genuine and warm. "And you're welcome, Faith. So, what do you have planned for the rest of the day?"

She gazed out the window, her eyes tracing the peaks and valleys as they rolled past in a quiet, comforting rhythm. "Honestly, I don't have much planned. I'll probably tinker with my bookcase for a bit or put on a movie. Or maybe I'll head over to the shop and get caught up on some work."

Ryan turned to her. "Faith... it's Easter Sunday. A day for something other than work. I don't have anyone waiting for me back home. I don't want the day to end yet."

Her heart gave a small, unexpected flutter at his confession, but she tilted her head, skepticism in her hazel eyes. "Why?"

"Why not?" he said simply, his tone so sincere it left her momentarily speechless.

"All right." Faith tapped her fingers absentmindedly on her thigh as she thought. "Well... my typical Sundays aren't exactly action-packed. Dad and I usually pop some popcorn and watch a couple of old movies, play board games... that sort of thing. It's nothing fancy." She paused, heat creeping up her neck as she added with a self-conscious laugh, "You're probably not interested in something as low-key as that."

Ryan didn't miss a beat. "Why not? I love board games." His hazel eyes flicked toward her before returning to the road. "And watching a movie sounds like a perfect way to end a day like this."

Faith blinked. "Wait... are you serious?"

"Completely." He smiled, his voice calm but steady. "You had me at board games."

A laugh bubbled up before she could contain it. "Okay, now I'm curious. What's your favorite? Let me guess—it's Monopoly, and you're ruthless about winning?"

"You wound me, Faith," he said with a dramatic hand to his chest. "Monopoly is awesome, Scrabble, just about any board game, really."

Faith grinned, shaking her head as she gestured toward an upcoming gravel road lined with tall sycamores. "Take the next turn like you're heading to the office, but when you hit the fork in the road, stick to the right."

He followed her direction. The truck crunched along the gravel path. "It's just a little farther, about half a mile down," Faith said.

As they rounded the bend, her childhood home came into view, framed by the backdrop of sunlit mountains and bordered by a picket fence. The sprawling property that carried three generations of Mc-Neil craftsmanship seemed to rise into sight like a promise born of time and care.

Ryan's breath caught as he eased the truck to a slower pace, his eyes immediately drawn to the stunning home nestled between the towering mountains. The golden tones of the warm cedar siding glowed softly in the late-afternoon light, framed perfectly by the lush greenery of the spring foliage. The porch stretched gracefully across the front of the house, its hand-turned posts and meticulously crafted railings a testament to timeless craftsmanship. A burgundy metal roof gleamed above, its color vivid against the backdrop of the rolling hills, while the neatly landscaped garden surrounding the house hinted at years of love and care. Everything about it, from the stone pathway leading to the front steps to the way the home seemed to blend effortlessly into its surroundings, felt intentional—as though it had grown alongside the trees themselves.

"Wow," he said simply, his voice tinged with awe. He glanced at her, his expression softening. "This is... incredible."

"Not bad, huh?" Faith said, directing him toward the garage. "Park over there. The stairs up to my apartment are on the side."

He pulled up in front of the garage and shut off the engine.

Faith motioned for him to follow, climbing the stairs to her apartment, while Ryan trailed behind. When she opened the door and stepped inside, she tried not to fidget as she waited for his reaction.

Ryan stepped through and stopped short, his eyes widening just slightly as he took it all in. "Faith..." he started, his gaze shifting from the exposed beams to the wide plank floors to the windows framing the mountain views like a painting. "This is... this is beautiful."

"I wanted it to feel like a private getaway," she said quietly, dismissing the pinch of nervousness in her tone. "Comfortable. A place I could enjoy."

Ryan's eyes swept across the space, taking in every detail with quiet admiration. The apartment exuded a charm uniquely Faith—warm and effortlessly inviting, with a meticulous attention to detail. The open-concept living area was bathed in natural light streaming through oversized windows, perfectly framing the undulating mountain ranges beyond. The view alone was enough to leave him momentarily speechless, as if the outside world had decided to pull up a chair by the picture-perfect panes.

The apartment's rustic elegance was a seamless blend of iron and wood. Industrial meets country chic. High, vaulted ceilings were crisscrossed with exposed wooden beams, their aged textures a testament to Faith's craftsmanship and love of detail. The wide plank floors, their sun-warmed tones rich and weathered, stretched throughout the space, grounding it in a timeless aesthetic that whispered of both beauty and functionality.

The kitchen caught his attention next—equal parts modern comfort and vintage nostalgia. Sleek, modern appliances blended effortlessly with the handcrafted cabinetry, their soft, sage-green hue a gentle nod to its rustic theme. Counters made from polished butcher block gleamed beneath the overhead lighting, while the backsplash of glazed subway tiles added a subtle, timeless charm. A cast-iron farmhouse sink stood proudly beneath another large window, framing yet another spectacular mountain view. The center island was a clear work of art, its sturdy, reclaimed wood base supporting a polished countertop.

A large, deep-set farmhouse table occupied one corner of the main space, flanked by mismatched chairs that somehow tied together, each painted in monochromatic shades of cream and willow. Above it hung a spherical iron chandelier, its Edison bulbs casting a soft, golden glow that warmed the room.

Ryan couldn't help but let his gaze drift toward the smaller, personal touches—wooden shelves filled with neatly stacked books, a small antique radio, and jars of dried herbs lining one wall like ornaments of a bygone era. A few framed photographs hung on the walls near the built-ins—black-and-white snapshots of a younger Faith with her father, and presumably her grandfather, tools in hand, beaming proudly. The sense of her legacy, the sheer weight and beauty of her family's history, was palpable in every corner.

The living room was no less impressive, with a stone fireplace anchoring one wall, complete with a live-edge wooden mantle above. More unique decor pieces showcased her personality, from intricate metal sconces to woven blankets carefully folded over the couch's arm. The cushions of the oversized sofa practically begged for someone to sink into them, and a pair of handmade wooden rocking chairs flanked the space—simple yet refined, a labor of love evident in their finishing details.

Ryan's appreciation grew with each passing second. "Faith, this place..." His voice trailed off for a moment as he continued to take it in, shaking his head slightly. "... It's incredible. Did you—?"

"Build it myself?" Faith asked with a grin, crossing her arms with a hint of playful pride. "Well, mostly. Dad and the crew helped with the heavier builds when I needed an extra set of hands. Everything else..." She shrugged, her voice softening. "Let's just say it was a labor of love."

"It's not just beautiful," Ryan said, sincerity lacing his tone. "It feels...alive. Like it's telling a story." His gaze lingered on the beams overhead. "And it's you through and through."

Faith felt a faint blush creep up her neck at his words, but she quickly brushed it off, motioning for Ryan to follow her further inside. "Come on. I hope you're ready to lose in whatever board game you pick because I'm unbeatable."

Ryan couldn't help feeling like he'd just stepped into a well-loved sanctuary—a place not just built with skill, but with heart. It was entirely Faith, and he wouldn't have imagined it any other way.

"So... Scrabble or Monopoly?" she asked.

"Monopoly all the way!"

Chapter 22

Faith stepped back, crossing her arms as she surveyed the newly completed wraparound porch. It framed the house beautifully, hugging it in a seamless loop that reminded her of a well-tailored jacket—practical, sturdy, yet undeniably charming. The warm evening light slid across the smooth boards, accentuating the faint sheen of the protective sealant her crew had applied yesterday. Every inch of the porch spoke volumes about the hours of precision, collaboration, and sweat her team had poured into this project. It wasn't her first big porch renovation, but it might just be her proudest to date.

The clapboard siding on the house that had stood weathered and war-torn by decades of Appalachian storms was now replaced with crisp white vinyl. Every line sat flush against the house like sheets carefully tucked on a freshly made bed, perfectly aligned. It was clean, modern, but still carried an air of the nostalgic charm that made this house special.

The new windows were another triumph. Initially, Faith had agonized over how to handle them. Some of the original ones were miraculously intact, their glass panes refracting light into the kind of imperfect rainbows only time could create. But cost-effectiveness won out in the end. Refurbishing them had proved to be a logistical nightmare—and a financial one, too. Ryan had weighed in on the decision, as pragmatic as ever, and she had begrudgingly conceded. Now, as she gazed at the bright, energy-efficient windows—double paned, sturdy, and framed with sleek, country-blue vinyl shutters—she couldn't help but admit he'd made the right choice. The shutters themselves were her suggestion, a last-minute addition that softened the home's otherwise classic Victorian edge.

And then there was the roof. The patchy remnants of the old slate tiles had been stripped away by roofing professionals Ryan had hired last week, replaced with a gleaming metal roof in a subtly shining shade of blue that nearly matched the shutters. The lines between the panels ran straight and true, corrugated to perfection, and Faith knew this roof would likely last another lifetime—or two.

Her gaze shifted back to the porch, where her team's craftsmanship was on full display. Her eyes scanned the precise latticework that wrapped the foundation. The railings were perfectly aligned, showcasing every squared baluster with meticulous spacing. This wasn't just a job done right; this was art. The two new porch swings were perhaps her favorite detail. They had been last-minute additions, insisted upon by Ryan. "You can't have a porch like this and no porch swings," he'd argued, with that roguish grin of his.

Ryan stepped through the front door, pausing to take it all in. His shirt clung to his torso, damp with sweat and dust from a long day of sanding floors inside. Stray wisps of dark hair fell across his forehead, evidence of a hard day's work, but none of it dimmed the effortless charm of his warm, easy smile.

"Well?" he said. "Is the house officially done on the outside, or are you going to find one more thing to fuss over?"

Faith smirked as she walked toward the porch. "I'm thinking the third baluster on the left could be a millimeter off," she teased, cocking her head theatrically.

Ryan laughed. "See, this is why people are afraid of you, Faith. No one is safe from your perfectionist tendencies."

"Afraid of me?" She said, one eyebrow arching in mock offense. "No one's afraid of me, Ryan. They just... respect my high standards."

"Tomato, tomahto," he retorted. "But seriously, you've outdone yourself. This is incredible."

"We outdid ourselves," she corrected, folding her arms again. "It wasn't just me out here with a hammer, you know."

"True," Ryan conceded. "But let's not kid ourselves—you're the reason this place looks as good as it does so far."

He set his tool belt down on the porch and glanced toward the nearest swing. "Care to test it out?" he asked, stepping toward the wooden seat and giving it a quick shake to emphasize its sturdiness.

"Absolutely."

Faith lowered herself onto the swing. She leaned back, letting the gentle sway of the swing coax her into a rare state of relaxation. Ryan joined her without asking, sitting down beside her on the swing's other end. The swing's chains creaked, but otherwise, the evening remained quiet, the sounds of the countryside filling the silence.

They sat there for a moment, neither of them speaking. Faith's gaze drifted outward, tracing the familiar contours of the land—the rolling hills, the old maples standing sentinel along the driveway, the soft amber-glow cast by the setting sun. Everything felt calm, like the world had taken a small, fleeting pause just for them.

"So," Ryan said. "What's next on the list?"

Faith smiled, closing her eyes for a moment before answering. "Getting through tomorrow without pulling my hair out," she quipped, though there was a thread of genuine exhaustion behind her words.

"You know, you could let yourself take a whole day off, Faith. Word on the street is it does wonders for the soul. And let's be honest—your crew has proven they can manage just fine without you micromanaging them."

Faith smirked, rolling her eyes, but unable to hide the small laugh that escaped. "I just might take the entire day off," she bantered back, her tone lighter than usual, though pointed enough to acknowledge her chronic reluctance to step away from work.

Ryan leaned back, the swing creaking softly under their combined weight. "Might not be a bad idea, especially with your dad coming home tomorrow. Something tells me you'll be juggling enough without throwing work into the mix."

Faith nodded, a small smile tugging at her lips. "Yeah, they're saying probably in the afternoon. After the doctor's morning rounds and the usual mountain of discharge paperwork. I could work in the morning."

"I vote you take the whole day off. Would you like some company for the trip?"

Faith tilted her head at Ryan, trying to gauge his intent. She hesitated, her first instinct to insist she could handle it on her own. But something stopped her—maybe it was the steady way he looked at her, like he'd already decided he wasn't taking no for an answer, but would let her pretend it was her choice, anyway.

"Company wouldn't be the worst thing," she admitted.

"How about this? We both take a break from work for the day," Ryan suggested, his tone warm and easy. "In the morning, we'll head to one of those big-box home improvement stores and pick out some fixtures for the kitchen and bathrooms. Then we can grab a quick lunch, and by that time, it'll probably be just about right to swing by and pick him up."

She looked at him, a small smile softening her features. "I like the way you think. While we're out, I want to pick up a few things for Dad's house. I've been meaning to install a grab bar in his bathroom; the last thing I need is for him to slip and fall getting out of the shower. Oh, and maybe we could swing by the bookstore too. Dad loves those old westerns. I'll grab a few to keep him occupied."

"Sounds like a plan," Ryan said after a pause. "What about after tomorrow?"

"One step at a time," she said, forcing her tone to stay even.

Ryan studied her, his smile softening around the edges. "Faith McNeil," he said thoughtfully, his voice unhurried, "you mean you don't have a solid plan in place."

She shook her head, a small smile playing on her lips despite herself. "No... honestly, I don't know what to expect from here. Dad's not as young as he used to be. His health isn't great, and I can't shake the feeling he's not telling me everything about it."

"Really?"

"Yes," she replied softly, her gaze drifting toward the porch rail, as if searching for answers in the smooth wood grain. "I think I'm stepping into that phase of life where it's my turn to look out for him. Keeping an eye on him, making sure he doesn't push himself too hard—it's going to be an adjustment."

Ryan studied her for a moment before speaking, his voice steady. "Do you think he'll retire?"

Faith let out a breath, a faint smile tugging at the corners of her lips, though it didn't quite reach her eyes. "Retire," she echoed, almost tasting the weight of the word. "That's the one thing I've been bracing myself for—like it's this inevitability we've both been dancing around. And honestly... yeah, I think that's where we're headed." Her voice dipped, a thread of hesitation woven through her words. "But knowing it's coming doesn't make it any easier to accept."

"Don't dread it," Ryan said, his voice calm and reassuring. "If he's decided to retire, it's something to celebrate. Not everyone gets the chance to step back and truly enjoy life. Think of it this way—he'll finally have more time for himself, more days to savor, and no more grueling hours at work weighing him down."

Faith turned to face him, searching his eyes as his words settled over her like a gentle breeze. She studied him for a long moment, as if seeing him anew, and before she could stop herself, the words tumbled free.

"You are not at all what I expected when we first met. You're different," she said.

Ryan turned his head toward her, one brow arching slightly. "Different how?"

She looked away quickly, staring down at the worn jeans covering her thighs. "I don't know," she muttered, her voice quieter now. "I just thought you'd be—" She stopped, realizing anything she said could either come off as insulting or embarrassing. "Never mind," she finished, shaking her head.

"No, no. Don't stop now," he prodded, and she could hear the smile in his voice. "You thought I'd be, what—obnoxious? Helpless? A clueless city boy trying to impress the locals?"

She bit her lip, trying to hold back her grin. "Something like that."

"Well," he said, his tone dipping into that playful lilt she'd come to enjoy, "lucky for you, I contain multitudes."

Faith chuckled, shaking her head at his antics. "You're ridiculous."

"And yet, here you are." He stretched his arms over his head, the shift in posture making the swings' chains creak. "Stuck with me—for at least a little while longer."

"I'm really glad you came into my life," Faith said, her voice steady but laced with quiet vulnerability. "I think facing this new chapter with my dad, and everything that comes with it, might be a little easier with you here."

Ryan's hazel eyes softened as he met her gaze. "The road ahead won't be easy, Faith," he said gently. "But try to be grateful for the chance to walk it with him."

His words landed deep, striking a chord she didn't often let herself dwell on. She felt a tight ache bloom in her chest, the kind that came with imagining the unthinkable, a life without her dad in it. It wasn't a thought she allowed herself to linger on, but in that moment, his words made her face it, even just for a heartbeat.

"What about you?" Faith asked, her tone soft and curious. "You don't talk much about your parents. What are they like?"

Ryan leaned back slightly, the corner of his mouth lifting in a faint smile, as if her question had tugged at a memory he wasn't entirely sure he wanted to unpack. His gaze drifted outward, settling somewhere beyond the horizon, before he began to speak.

"My parents... they truly are remarkable," Ryan began, his voice carrying a mix of admiration and something harder to define, like the edges of pride softened by distant memories. "Take my mom, Margaret—or Meg, as everyone calls her. She's brilliant, honestly. A leading cardiovascular researcher, internationally renowned for what she does. Her name's on studies people cite in journals. But expressing emotions or showing warmth or love? That's not really her thing. She's nurturing, I guess, in her own way, but she's not the type to dole out words of encouragement or wrap you in hugs when you're down.

It's not that she's unkind; she's just... different. Growing up with her wasn't bad, not at all. It just wasn't what you'd call traditional. You know how some moms have this effortless way of making you feel like the center of their world? That wasn't her style."

Faith tilted her head slightly, her soft features reflecting interest and curiosity, though she didn't interrupt.

"And my dad, Tom, he's... well, let's just say no one forgets meeting Tom Dalton. He's brilliant, too. A professor of economics, a leader in rural development research, sharp as a tack and quick with a dry sense of humor that sneaks up on you. He's practical to a fault and probably one of the hardest workers I've ever known. But let's just say his way of showing affection involved a lot of lectures about life lessons, sometimes on things that were way over my head... or honestly didn't matter to me. Which was fine—I did learn a lot from him. But emotional connection? It wasn't exactly his strong suit, either."

Faith's eyebrows drew together faintly. "Were they... distant?"

"Not intentionally, no, I think it's part of who they are," Ryan said with a small shrug. "They always cared in their own way—they still do. But they're both workaholics, and growing up, they were laser-focused on their careers. There were times when I couldn't shake the feeling that I was... an afterthought. Not because they didn't love me, but because their goals and ambitions always seemed to take precedence. If I ever needed real emotional grounding or that sense of being truly seen and loved, it wasn't coming from them. It came from my grandparents."

"That's why you were so close to them," she said, more a realization than a question.

Ryan nodded, a soft, almost wistful smile forming. "Yeah. My grandparents were special people. Steady, present, patient. They had this way of making you feel like, no matter what you were dealing with, you had a safe place to land. You knew you were loved and wanted when you were around them. I spent so much of my childhood here with them, all of my summer and holiday breaks from school, just every spare moment I could... and those times were the best parts of my childhood. I didn't feel like I had to compete with a research project or a university board meeting for their attention. They ... they just showed up for me."

Faith studied him for a moment, her arms loosely crossed over her knees. "It sounds like they gave you something your parents couldn't."

"Exactly." Ryan's voice deepened, carrying a hint of emotion that hadn't been there before. "And that's stuck with me, you know? My grandparents weren't flashy or ambitious, but they were present in a way my parents never really were. Don't get me wrong—I don't resent my parents for how they are. I understand now that I'm an adult. They are who they are. But it taught me something important. I don't want to be that kind of parent. If God blesses me with kids, I want them to know—without a doubt—that they're my priority. That I'll be present for them, not just in a practical sense, but emotionally, too."

Faith smiled but didn't say anything, sensing there was more he wanted to say.

Ryan ran a hand through his hair, his hazel eyes clouded with thought. "Honestly, leaving my corporate job in Chicago is something my parents don't really get it. They're struggling with it. They supported my decision on the surface—they'd never come out and say they were disappointed in me, but I can feel it. They think I threw away something important. And the truth is..." He paused, his gaze flicking toward Faith, "I did throw something away—on purpose."

Faith tilted her head.

"They don't understand why I'd trade a huge salary, a clear career path, and a corner office in a high rise for... this," he said, gesturing toward the sprawling countryside around them. "To them, success is climbing the corporate ladder or being the best in your field. And for them? Maybe that's true. But for me? Success looks different. I don't want to become so consumed by work that I forget to live. I want to build something that matters—not just to me, but to the people around me. I want to have a family someday, and I want to be able to look my kids in the eye and know that I chose a life where they could see what really matters."

"That's why this farmhouse is so important to me," he continued, "It's not just a business venture—it's a statement about the kind of life I want to live. I want that balance my grandparents had. I want to be present for the people who matter to me. I don't want to be the kind of dad who stays buried in spreadsheets or research deadlines while his kids' lives pass by in the background."

Faith shifted slightly, her expression contemplative but touched with a quiet smile.

"Sounds like you're breaking the cycle," she said softly, her voice carrying a blend of admiration and quiet wonder.

Ryan looked at her, the faintest smile tugging at the corners of his mouth. "I'm trying. I'm a work in progress. I definitely don't have it all figured out, but... I'm giving it my best shot."

"How did you become such a good man, Ryan? Honestly... your kind of amazing."

Surprised by her candor, he turned to meet her gaze fully, his voice steady, yet tinged with humility. "By the grace of God, Faith. Nothing else explains it."

Chapter 23

Faith slid the serving bowl onto the round dining table, catching a whiff of the savory stir-fry Ryan had spent the better part of an hour preparing. The scent was amazing, ginger and garlic mingling together with the light tang of soy sauce. She adjusted the napkin by her father's plate, feeling the slight pull in her lower back, the lingering result of a long day. But James was home now, and that was all that mattered.

Ryan set the steaming wok down on a folded kitchen towel in the center of the table, his sleeves rolled up to his elbows.

"Alright," Ryan said with a hint of pride. "Might not be five-star, but it's edible. I think."

James chuckled, his gravelly laugh making Faith's heart lift. Just days ago, he'd been pale and weak in a hospital bed, and now he was here with them, bright-eyed and more himself than he had been in weeks.

"Well," James began, reaching for the serving spoon, "if this tastes as good as it smells, I'd say you're a keeper."

Ryan's grin was easy, and Faith caught herself smiling as she took a seat next to her dad. It was strange how quickly Ryan had blended into their little world, how natural it had become for him to be here—cooking a meal, teasing her, lending a steadying hand when her own felt shaky.

"It's just stir-fry," Ryan said modestly, scooping a portion onto his plate. "Nothing fancy."

James jabbed his fork in Ryan's direction. "Don't you dare downplay a good meal. You know, Faith never cooked for me like this."

"Oh, come on, Dad," Faith said, rolling her eyes. "I made lasagna. Twice."

"Burnt lasagna doesn't count," James shot back, shaking his head.

Faith gasped, feigning offense. "I'll have you know, I lovingly assembled that lasagna from scratch—and only half the noodles were... a little tough."

Ryan chuckled, his mouth tugging into a crooked smile. "Remind me to keep you out of the kitchen, then."

Faith reached for her glass of water, trying to hide her grin. She enjoyed seeing them like this—James and Ryan exchanging easy banter, her dad looking better and happier. For a moment, it almost felt like their lives were untouched by burdens, as if the worries and hardships of the past few weeks had been pushed into the background.

They ate together, laughter and conversation filling Faith's childhood home. James took playful swings at Ryan's cooking, which only encouraged Ryan to pile more vegetables onto his plate, declaring, "Carrots are good for your eyesight—I'm keeping you around for the long haul, James."

As the plates began to empty and the room fell into a steady rhythm of forks clinking against plates, James cleared his throat. The shift was almost imperceptible, like a change in the wind. Faith glanced at him, her stomach tightening instinctively. His smile had faded, replaced by a shadow of something she couldn't quite name.

"Faith," he said, setting his fork down and leaning back slightly. "We need to talk after dinner."

Her pulse stuttered. There was no mistaking the determined edge in his voice. She wiped her hands on her napkin, trying to think of a way to steer the conversation anywhere but where it was evidently headed. "Talk? About what? I mean, we've been talking all evening, haven't we? Maybe this can wait—"

"Faith," James interrupted gently, but firmly, giving her a look that was both kind and immovable. "This isn't something we can keep brushing off."

Her cheeks flushed slightly as she stared at her plate. She could feel Ryan's gaze on her, quiet but observant, like he was trying to piece together what was happening. She opened her mouth, a protest on the tip of her tongue, but James wasn't finished.

He turned to Ryan now, eyebrows raised. "You mentioned before you have a background in finances, right?"

Ryan blinked, clearly surprised. "Uh, yeah. I was a financial analyst. Why?"

James nodded, as if that were all he needed to hear. "That'll do. I need your help. Are you okay with being a part of this discussion?"

Ryan's gaze shifted briefly to Faith, carefully skimming her expression, as though gauging whether his involvement would upset her. But Faith kept her head down, unable to meet his eyes.

"Of course," Ryan said finally. There was no hesitation in his voice, no uncertainty. "If it's important to you, I'm happy to stay."

Faith's throat tightened, and she looked at her father sharply. "Dad, this doesn't need to involve him," she said quietly, almost pleadingly. "Can't this just wait until tomorrow?"

James shook his head and calmly wiped his mouth with his napkin. "Faith, whether you like it or not, no, it can't wait any longer."

Faith's lips parted like she was going to say something—anything—but she simply exhaled, her shoulders sagging in resignation.

Ryan cleared his throat. "I'll help however I can," he said, looking at Faith briefly before shifting his attention back to James. For someone who'd walked into this family's orbit just weeks ago, his steadiness felt like a lifeline.

Dinner wrapped up quietly after that. Faith carried her plate to the sink, the routine movements of rinsing and stacking dishes in the dishwasher momentarily grounding her in the normalcy of the moment. Ryan appeared beside her, his movements effortless as he helped. "You don't have to stay," she said.

"I want to," Ryan replied simply. "Whatever's going on, we'll figure it out."

She glanced at him. It was a small moment, but his presence felt reassuring, like she didn't have to carry what was coming next alone.

When the dishes were finally done, Faith turned toward her dad, who now sat quietly at the dining table. In front of him was a worn manila folder, and the notebook he had written in while in the hospital. Something about the way his hands rested protectively on them made her stomach churn.

"Alright," Faith said softly, sitting beside him. Ryan took the seat next to her. "What's this about, Dad?"

James leaned forward, his expression heavy with emotion. "We need to talk about me. About my retirement, about this house, the business, and a few other things."

Faith stilled, the blood draining slightly from her face.

Chapter 24

James shifted in his chair, adjusting his reading glasses as he opened the notebook, his roughened fingers gripping the edges like it held something sacred. Clearing his throat, he looked at Faith with an expression that was calm but resolute.

"Retirement," he began, his deep voice cutting through the silence of the dining room, "I never thought I'd have to make this decision so soon, but here we are."

Faith blinked. Retire? Her father? The man who had spent his entire life working from dawn until the stars came out? The idea was absurd, but she had known it was coming.

"Dad," she blurted, her voice rising, "you don't have to do this. You've been through a lot, I get that, but take a few months off. Rest. Go fishing or... or do some gardening or something. But why retire? It just sounds so final." Her words tumbled out faster than she could catch them, the pitch of her voice betraying her panic.

James gave her a small, fond smile, the kind that said he'd already expected every word she was about to say. He reached across the table and patted her hand, his touch surprisingly gentle for a man whose hands had built entire homes.

"Honey," he said softly, "I've made up my mind."

Faith's throat tightened, and she yanked her hand back, folding her arms defensively across her chest. "Why do you always do this?" she said, her tone sharper now. "You make these big decisions, and then you just expect me to go along with them like it's nothing? You don't even ask—"

"This isn't about you agreeing or disagreeing," James interrupted, his voice steady but insistent. "This is about reality. And the reality is, my heart isn't what it used to be."

Ryan, sitting quietly like a steady presence at her side, glanced between them, his hazel eyes flickering with concern. Faith felt his gaze on her, but she chose to ignore it, her eye contact locked tightly onto her father.

"You said you're feeling better," she argued, her voice trembling at the edges. "You said you plan to start eating healthier. You promised to follow the doctor's orders, Dad! How can you sit here and act like everything needs to come to an end?"

James leaned back in his chair, exhaling a deep breath. He took his glasses off, setting them gently on the table before rubbing the bridge of his nose. It was the face of a man who'd lived a thousand lives in one, weathered and wise but weary all the same.

"Faith," he said, his tone tender but unrelenting. "I want you to listen to me. Really listen. Dr. Benson didn't mince her words. The damage to my heart... it's not going away. Sure, the meds are helping, but even with them, my health is terrible, and it's not going to get much better anytime soon. Do you have any idea what that actually means?"

Her lip quivered, but she didn't respond. She couldn't.

"It means," James continued, "if I keep trying to live the way I've always lived—working twelve-hour days, climbing scaffolding, hauling lumber—I won't be around much longer. And while the thought of going home to be with the Lord does not scare me, it terrifies me to think of leaving things undone. Leaving you unprepared."

Faith opened her mouth, but no words came. The room felt too warm.

James flipped open the notebook and scanned some of his notes. "I've already set up an appointment for tomorrow afternoon," he said, his voice matter-of-fact, as though they were discussing roof repairs. "The lawyer's coming here to the house. We're putting everything in order—my will, the business, the house. Everything."

Faith's heart thudded painfully in her chest. "You don't need to do this now," she whispered, her voice shaking. "There's time. We have time."

James gave her a sad smile. "Honey, if there's one thing this old heart of mine has taught me, it's that waiting for tomorrow doesn't always work out the way you think it will. I need to know that when my time comes, you're taken care of. That the company is in the right hands."

"You're not dying," Faith snapped, her voice rising again. "Stop talking like you're already gone!"

James reached across the table again, gripping her hand firmly this time. His eyes, tired but unflinching, locked onto hers. "I'm not giving up," he said simply. "But I'm being honest, Faith. There's a difference. And honesty means making sure everything's squared away now, not later."

James turned his attention to Ryan, his somber expression lifting just slightly. "Now, you're good with numbers, right?"

"I'd like to think so," he said. "It's kind of what I used to do for a living."

"Well, you'll have to forgive me," James said, leaning back in his chair again. "I've never been one for understanding what a financial analyst actually does. Sounds like one of those fancy titles people in suits throw around. But I do know the books over at McNeil Construction could use a fresh set of eyes."

Ryan's brows furrowed slightly. "You want me to look at the financials?"

James nodded. "That's what I'm asking. Monica and Tom have been keeping things running, but I've never been much good at numbers myself. If anything's out of place or if there's anything we could be doing better, I'd like to know. And I trust you more than I'd trust a banker who's never set foot on a job site."

Faith glanced at Ryan, who met her gaze briefly, a flicker of uncertainty crossing his face. "I'd be happy to help," he said, turning back to James. "I can take a look at everything and let you know what I find."

"Good man," James said, a hint of relief in his voice. "Lord knows, I've been putting that off for too long."

Faith felt herself sinking lower into her chair, the weight of the moment pressing down on her like an unbearable heat. She wanted to be angry at Ryan for agreeing so easily, but she couldn't. He looked calm, steady—even eager to help. And maybe a small part of her was relieved that she didn't have to do this part on her own. Still, the knot in her stomach twisted tighter when James turned his attention back to her.

"The lawyer will be here around two tomorrow," he said. "But I'll need you to grab a few things from the office in the morning before you head out to Ryan's place to work."

Faith frowned. "What things?"

James reached into his pocket and pulled out a folded piece of paper, sliding it across the table. "It's all on this list. The original company charter, a few things from my office, a box of rolled-up blue-prints—should be under the drafting table—and the current ledger Monica keeps in the bottom drawer of her desk."

Faith unfolded the paper, her eyes scanning the list despite the fact that her brain was screaming to protest again. "The charter? Why do you need that?"

"Let's just call it tying up loose ends," James replied, his tone as firm as the set of his jaw.

Her eyes burned as they lingered on the piece of paper. Fighting him on this was useless. He wasn't going to budge, and deep down, she knew he was right to prepare. But that didn't make it any less painful. "Fine," she said finally, shoving the paper into her pocket.

James smiled, the tension in his face softening as he leaned back with a sigh. "Thank you, honey."

Faith didn't reply. She couldn't. Words felt too big and too small all at once, and the lump in her throat made it hard to breathe. She stood abruptly, muttering something about needing a quick break.

Ryan followed her into the kitchen, his movements unassuming but deliberate. He stood beside her at the sink as she stared out the window into the darkness.

"This is a lot," she finally whispered, breaking the silence without looking at him.

"It is," he agreed, his tone quiet and measured. "But it's what your father wants."

Her laugh was bitter, almost involuntary. "Yeah? Well, what about me?"

Ryan didn't respond right away. He just watched her. "One step at a time, okay? Everything is going to work out just fine. This is a lot right now, and I get that," he said gently. "Listen to your dad, do as he says. Can you do that?"

Faith looked up at him, on the verge of tears, and nodded.

Chapter 25

Faith flipped the light switch on, pausing in the doorway of her father's office as she surveyed the room. It felt untouched, frozen in time since the last time she had stepped inside. The desk, scarred with years of wear, bore its familiar constellation of coffee rings—blemishes that told stories of early mornings and late nights. Behind it, the battered leather chair sat waiting, its cushion bearing the unmistakable imprint of James McNeil. It was more than just a chair; it was a quiet witness to decades of determination, hours spent meticulously reviewing construction bids, blueprints, and schedules. Faith inhaled deeply, the faint scent of sawdust and old paper tugging at memories both comforting and bittersweet.

She placed the stack of documents and blueprints she had gathered so far carefully on her father's desk, then pulled the folded list from her pocket to double-check her progress. The rolled blueprints from under the drafting table? Check. The rest of the items on the list seemed manageable. For now, it was just a matter of navigating her dad's filing cabinet to locate the remaining things on his list.

Faith drew in a measured breath, her heart heavier than her task list. She'd barely slept after last night's conversation. Her father's words still pressed down on her like a physical force: "Retirement. Putting my affairs in order. When my time comes."

She wasn't ready for this. Not for the responsibility, not for his retirement he seemed so determined to plan for, and certainly not for the possibility of him leaving this earth. Yet here she was, digging through blueprints and sorting paperwork like it was just another project to tackle and not the emotional minefield that it truly was.

The filing cabinet loomed in the far corner of the office, a battered relic of years gone by. Its steel surface bore the scars of time—scratches, dents, and the faint smudges of fingerprints that no amount of cleaning could erase. Faith stood before it, the room around her hushed but for the steady hum of the fluorescent light above. Taking a slow breath, she gripped the handle of the top drawer and eased it open.

Her eyes roved over the neat row of file tabs, their faded labels a testament to their constant handling. It didn't take long to spot one of the items on her father's list. She tugged it free and set it on the desk.

Moving to the second drawer, she pulled it open with a sharp metallic creak. She scanned its contents quickly but came up empty. A flicker of irritation crossed her face. She crouched and reached for the third drawer, her fingers tightening around the handle. The groan of metal on metal filled the room as it reluctantly slid open.

Inside, she found another file her dad wanted, its tab slightly bent from years of wear. Lowering herself to the cool tile floor, she grabbed the handle of the bottom drawer and gave it a determined pull. The drawer resisted, the groan louder this time, as though protesting its own age and overuse. She peered inside and was greeted by an orderly line of folders, their tabs standing at perfect attention like soldiers awaiting review.

Her finger skimmed the labels one by one. Permits. Client Contracts. Supplier Invoices. Her lips moved silently as she read. There it was—Charter. Bright letters handwritten across the tab, stark against the yellowed folder.

Faith exhaled, a mixture of relief and resignation washing over her. She pulled the folder out gently, holding it in her hands as though it were something precious. Rising to her feet with steady resolve, she set her jaw and placed the last two file folders on the desk.

"Well, that was easy," she muttered to herself.

Maybe this morning won't be as bad as I thought.

She turned back to the filing cabinet and bent over to close the drawer, and she noticed several bulky files in the back, unlabeled. Faith hesitated, biting the inside of her cheek. Technically, she had everything she needed from her dad's list, but her curiosity got the best of her. She pulled the folders out and carried them to her father's desk.

She slid into his chair; the leather creaking softly beneath her weight, and placed the folders in front of her. When she flipped the top folder open, her breath caught in her throat.

Photographs. Documents. All connected to one person.

Her mother.

There was a copy of her mother's social security card, next to a grainy black-and-white copy of her driver's license. Faith barely recognized the woman in the photo. Her mother's features were sharp and youthful, her hair swept into an elegant style that seemed completely out of place compared to the disheveled memories Faith carried of her.

A copy of a life insurance policy followed, along with an old, yellowed marriage license. Faith's hands trembled as she flipped through each piece of paper, her gaze lingering on a photo tucked toward the back. It showed her mother, smiling, holding a wide-eyed toddler in her arms. They were on the front porch of her dad's house.

Faith's chest tightened. She couldn't remember this moment—she couldn't even remember a time when her mother had looked this happy. The woman in this photograph wasn't the same person who had walked out on her and her dad all those years ago. That woman had been hard-edged, distracted, and desperate to leave. But this? This was someone entirely different.

Her fingers hovered over the picture for a moment longer before she carefully slid it back into the folder. She didn't trust herself to linger on it any longer without crumpling it and tossing it in the garbage.

The second file was thicker, and it hit her just as hard. The first document was a billing statement from a treatment facility specializing in addiction recovery. Faith's brow furrowed as she scanned the letterhead at the top. The invoice was addressed to her father, dated just a year after her mother walked out of their lives. Her eyes darted further down the page, and then further still, as she flipped through what seemed like dozens of similar statements, all stamped PAID.

Each bill had a check stapled to it, and every check bore her father's precise, looping signature.

Faith leaned back in the chair, the realization slamming into her like a rogue wave. Her mother had been in rehab. For drugs. For alcohol. Her father had paid for it, quietly and consistently, without ever breathing a word of it to Faith.

She stared at the words on the documents, her mind circling the same questions over and over: Why didn't he tell me? Did he think I wouldn't understand? Or did he just not want me to know?

It was too much to process, but something told her she wasn't done yet. She reached for the third and final file, bracing herself for what might come next.

The newspaper clippings were the first to fall out, their brittle edges curling as though they wanted to hide their contents from her. But

Faith read them anyway, her stomach twisting with every word she absorbed.

The articles told a story of a woman who had fallen even further after leaving rehab. Her mother, Faith realized, had become entangled in drug-dealing circles. One deal had gone horribly wrong, leading to a fight that ended with a man's death. Her mother was convicted of second-degree murder and sentenced to life in prison.

Faith's hands shook as she scanned the final clipping—an obituary dated 4 years after she had left her and her father. Faith would have been eighteen. It was brief, stating only her mother's name, her age, and that she had passed away peacefully in her sleep at the Franklin County Women's Correctional Facility. A check made out to a local funeral home in Ohio was stapled to the corner, once again signed by her father.

The chair creaked as Faith leaned forward, her elbows resting on the desk as she pressed the heels of her hands into her eyes. She couldn't breathe, couldn't think. The woman who had haunted her for so long—the woman whose absence had shaped so much of her life—had been carrying sins and struggles Faith had never even imagined. And her father had carried all of it alone.

"She's dead," she said.

Faith's hands fell to the desk, and her gaze drifted toward the window. The mountains that surrounded Laurel Ridge stood resolute in the distance, steady and unflinching despite the storm building inside her.

"Why?" she whispered, her voice cracking. "Why God didn't You... fix her? Help her? Help me?"

The silence, as always, offered no easy answers.

Chapter 26

Faith sat motionless in her father's chair, the folders splayed open on the desk in front of her like an exposed wound. Her fingers hovered over the edges of the papers, unsure whether to gather them up and toss them in the trash or shove them back into the drawer where they had been buried for so many years. Everything felt raw—her mother's face staring up at her from an old photograph, the cold finality of the obituary, the relentless trail of receipts and medical bills her father had paid without a word. It churned inside her, a whirlwind of anger, sadness, and something far more terrifying: doubt.

Why hadn't he told her? Why had he carried all of this alone, letting her believe her mother had just vanished without a backward glance, never to be heard from again? Why had God—who was supposed to be good and faithful—allowed her mother to spiral so completely into addiction and crime? A knot formed in her throat, tight and unyielding, as she stared blankly at the files.

The knock at the door jarred her from her spiraling thoughts. Faith blinked, startled, as Tom Davidson's voice cut through the quiet.

"Faith?"

She looked up sharply to see him standing in the doorway, his face shadowed with concern. He hesitated, lingering, as though sensing something wasn't quite right. "I saw the light on. Thought maybe your dad came in."

"Oh," Faith said, her voice tight as she quickly began stacking the folders, trying to keep her hands steady. "No, it's just me."

Tom stepped fully into the room, his sharp foreman's eyes scanning her face with that uncanny intuition of his. "How's he doing? James, I mean."

Faith hesitated, then plastered on a small smile she wasn't sure would convince him. "He's doing good," she said lightly, sliding the last folder into the pile and standing abruptly. "He's taking it easy, following the doctor's orders."

Tom nodded slowly, but his brow furrowed. "You sure you're okay? You look…" He trailed off, his tone careful, like he was treading on thin ice.

"I'm fine," she interrupted, her words sharper than she intended. She softened her tone almost immediately. "Really. I just—there's a lot to do this morning, and I need your help with something."

Tom crossed his arms, clearly not buying her casual dismissal, but wise enough to let it go for the moment. "What do you need?"

Faith turned back to the desk, gathering the files and blueprints her father wanted, and slid them into a beat-up leather portfolio bag. "I need you to take these up to my dad at the house." She handed the bag to Tom, who took it without protest but with a questioning look.

"Also," she added, snapping her fingers as though just remembering, "He wants the ledger from Monica's desk. It's in the bottom drawer. Can you grab that and bring it to him, too?"

Tom shifted the bag in his hands, his gaze still locked on her. "Sure. But are you sure you don't want me to—?"

"I'm fine," she said again, cutting him off more firmly this time. "Just take those things up to my dad, come back here, and wait for the crew. I'm taking the morning off."

Tom's eyebrows shot up. Faith taking more time off? She rarely even took Sundays off. She was always here, always working, always in control. "The morning off?" he repeated, his voice tinged with surprise and concern.

"Yes," she said, her tone brooking no argument. "I'll see you and the crew later today. Everything's fine."

He stood there for a beat longer, clearly debating whether to press the issue. Finally, he gave a small nod, though his eyes remained watchful. "All right," he said slowly. "But if you need anything..."

"I'll let you know," Faith replied quickly.

Tom lingered for a moment, then he nodded again and walked toward the door. Before he left, he paused, glancing back at her. "You know you can talk to me, Faith. About anything. Just... putting that out there."

Her heart twisted at the sincerity in his voice, but she forced another tight smile. "Thanks, Tom."

He gave her one last look, a mixture of concern and resignation, before leaving. Faith stood frozen for a moment.

When she was certain Tom was not coming back, she grabbed the folders about her mother and walked down the hall to her own office. Once inside, she closed the door firmly and locked it, leaning against it for a moment as she exhaled a shaky breath.

The familiarity of her office wrapped around her like a protective cocoon—the shelves lined with wood samples and tools, the drafting table covered in blueprints and notes. It was a space she had built for herself, a space where she was in control. But today, it felt like a stranger's room.

Faith moved to her desk and sank into the chair, placing the folders in front of her. Her hands trembled as she flipped the first one open again, the contents staring back at her like ghosts from another life.

The photos. Her mother's smile, so radiant and full of life, stared back at her from the weathered black-and-white snapshot. Faith's chest tightened as she traced the outline of her mother's face with her eyes, trying to reconcile the woman in the photos with the woman she remembered.

She shuffled through the stack, pausing on the picture of her mother holding her as a toddler. Faith's tiny hands rested on her mother's shoulder, her wide eyes staring directly into the camera. The juxtaposition of happiness and heartbreak in the image was almost unbearable.

"How could you leave?" she whispered, her voice breaking. "How could you do this to us?"

Her phone buzzed on the desk, jolting her. She glanced at the screen and saw Ryan's name flashing. His text was short and sweet: "Hey, just wanted to see how your morning was going. Let me know when you're on your way."

Faith stared at the screen for a long moment before flipping the phone over, muffling the vibration as another message followed. She couldn't deal with Ryan right now.

Instead, she focused back on the folders, pulling out the treatment facility bills and the obituary. Her father's signature, neat and looping, stared back at her from every check, a silent testament to the burden he had carried alone.

A sob escaped before she could stop it, raw and jagged. She pressed her palms to her face, trying to push the emotions back down where they belonged. But they refused to be buried this time.

"God," she whispered, her voice trembling, "I don't understand. I don't understand why you let this happen. To her. To us."

The silence that followed was deafening, offering no answers, no comfort.

Faith wiped her eyes and forced herself to keep going, flipping through the pages like they held some hidden truth she had missed. But all they offered was more heartache—more evidence of a life fractured by addiction and bad choices.

She leaned back in her chair, her eyes drifting to the ceiling as her thoughts spiraled. Her mother's death felt like a thief, stealing even the possibility of closure. And her father's silence... was it love? Protection? Or fear of what she might think if she knew the truth?

Her phone buzzed again. She ignored it.

Chapter 27

Faith's truck idled for a moment longer than necessary as she sat parked in front of the garage. The folders on the passenger seat loomed like an accusation, the contents within heavy with truths she wasn't sure she wanted to believe. Her fingers drummed against the steering wheel, her lower lip caught between her teeth. She had no plan. No grand strategy for what came next. For now, she just needed to breathe.

Pulling the keys from the ignition, she glanced at the folders one last time. Her chest tightening. With a quick shake of her head, she left them where they sat, grabbed her phone from the cupholder, and climbed out of the truck. The morning air was crisp and warm. She paused for a second, inhaling deeply, trying to clear her head. But no amount of fresh air could untangle the knot in her chest.

"Dad?" she called softly, as she stepped inside her childhood home.

"I'm in here," James's voice came from the dining room, steady and calm.

She found him exactly as she expected: seated at the head of the table, glasses perched on the bridge of his nose, a Bible spread open before him. A steaming mug of coffee sat within arm's reach.

James looked up as she entered, his eyes crinkling with a small smile. "Morning, sweetheart."

"Morning," she replied. She slid into the chair beside him, her hands fidgeting with the hem of her work shirt.

"You heading to Ryan's soon?" he asked.

"Yes. Just thought I'd stop and check to see if you needed anything."

"I'm fine. Don't need a thing. Just going to read my bible for a bit, then I'll probably read one of those westerns you picked up for me at the bookstore."

She nodded, her gaze briefly dropping to the Bible. His faith was so steady, so unwavering. It was like the foundation of one of their builds—solid, unshakable, and built to withstand storms. She envied it.

She leaned back in the chair. "So, you feel okay today? "

James set his coffee down, his expression turning serious but not heavy. "Better. A little tired, but I'll take that over what I've been through." He hesitated, then added, "Faith, you don't need to worry. I'll be fine. Gone on now and head to work."

"I will in a little bit," she said, her voice quieter.

He studied her for a moment, his gaze sharp and perceptive. "You okay, Faith? You seem a little preoccupied."

Her stomach twisted, but she kept her expression neutral. "I'm fine, Dad. Just a lot on my plate, that's all."

He didn't look convinced, but he didn't push. Instead, he leaned back in his chair, rubbing a hand over his chin. "Well, you know where to find me if you need to talk. About anything."

She nodded, swallowing hard against the lump rising in her throat. "You'll be right here. Promise me you won't get in your truck and go to the office or anywhere else. Just stay home and take it easy."

"Promise," he said.

Faith stood, smoothing her shirt. "I'm heading to Ryan's then. If you need me, just call or text, okay?"

James smiled, his eyes warm. "Will do. You have a good day, sweetheart."

"I will," she promised, though she wasn't entirely sure it was the truth.

***

As Faith drove toward Ryan's house, her hands gripped the steering wheel tighter than necessary, her knuckles paling under the pressure. The morning's revelations churned inside her, refusing to settle. Emotions, sharp and conflicting, battled for dominance. Anger surged first, hot and insistent, followed swiftly by confusion, betrayal, and an aching sadness she couldn't shake.

A part of her couldn't blame her father for keeping everything hidden. He had probably thought he was protecting her, sparing her from pain. But another part, a louder, angrier part, couldn't help but feel betrayed. If she couldn't trust her father, then who could she trust? The thought echoed in her mind, leaving her chest hollow.

The road blurred ahead of her as she replayed everything she'd read. Each piece of her mother's story carried with it an unbearable weight. Rehabilitation centers, addiction, a criminal record, and, finally, death.

"Why didn't he tell me? I had a right to know," Faith thought bitterly. But even as the anger flared, a quieter, guiltier voice whispered back: *"Would it have changed anything?"*

Faith shook her head, trying to focus on the winding mountain road.

"I shouldn't have looked." The thought was bitter, biting. If she had just shut the drawer, if she had just followed the list from her dad and ignored the tug of curiosity, she wouldn't be here now, caught in the middle of emotions she didn't want to face.

The truck's tires crunched over the gravel as she pulled off to the side of the road, too overwhelmed to drive another mile. She threw the gear into park and leaned forward, resting her forehead against the steering wheel as her thoughts spiraled, unrelenting.

"I didn't ask for this," she muttered, her voice cracking in the empty cab. "I didn't ask for any of this."

Her chest tightened as the morning's discoveries looped through her mind again. The faded photographs. The invoices from rehab. Check's her father had written. And then the obituary—short, cold, final.

Faith squeezed her eyes shut, but her mother's grainy photo was burned into her mind. The woman in the image wasn't the mother she remembered. It wasn't the woman who had walked out on her and her dad when she was fourteen. That woman had been broken, distant, and sharp-edged, as if life had sanded her down to her most jagged parts.

A shuddering breath escaped her as her anger began to ebb, replaced by a suffocating sadness. Maybe that's why her father hadn't told her. Maybe he had wanted to protect that fragile image he thought she had of her mother. Maybe he had been trying to spare her from the hurt and shame of all this, from the truth of who her mother had become.

But now, Faith wasn't sure what hurt more: the truth itself or the fact that her father had carried it alone, silently, for so long.

A buzzing from the cupholder pulled her from her thoughts. Faith blinked, disoriented, and glanced at her phone. Ryan's name lit up the screen. She let it ring, ignoring him for the third time that morning. She wasn't ready to talk to him yet—not when her emotions were this raw.

The phone fell silent, only to buzz again moments later with a text message. "You okay? Haven't heard from you. Let me know if you need anything."

Faith sighed. She couldn't bring herself to lean on Ryan, no matter how much she wanted to. This was her burden to carry, her mess to unravel.

"I don't need anyone. I can handle this," she told herself firmly, though the ache in her chest begged to differ.

The mountain air filtered through the slightly cracked window, brisk and grounding. Taking a deep breath, Faith started the truck again, determined to pull herself together.

As she turned back onto the road, her mind drifted to Ryan. His own backstory with his parents wasn't free of pain; she knew that much. Maybe he could help her understand all this. Or maybe he'd only see the cracks in her facade, the flaws she worked so hard to hide. The thought unsettled her, but she pushed it aside.

The farmhouse appeared as Faith crested the hill. Her crew's trucks were lined up in neat rows along the driveway.

Ryan sat on the front porch swing, his long legs stretched out in front of him. He glanced up just as Faith climbed out of her truck, her movements brisk, her expression unreadable beneath. His easy smile faltered, barely perceptible, but enough to betray his concern.

"Hey," he called, his tone cautious. "Everything okay?"

She hesitated, her hand lingering on the truck door as though it might anchor her. For a moment, she said nothing. Finally, she let out a shallow breath and walked toward the house. "No," she admitted. "Everything's not okay. But... it will be, eventually."

Ryan straightened, his expression softening with concern, but he didn't press her. He simply nodded, his gaze steady as it rested on her. "All right," he said gently. "I trust you."

"The countertops are on the way," he added. "They should be here any minute."

"Great," Faith replied, brushing a stray lock of hair from her face. Her tone was clipped, but not unkind, more matter-of-fact than anything else. "I'm heading upstairs to work with my crew. I'll send Tom and Mike down to help you with the install."

"Okay," Ryan said, tilting his head slightly as he studied her. "Faith, I was hoping you might help me with the install."

"No," she replied firmly, her hazel eyes meeting his with unwavering resolve. She wasn't about to crumble—not here, not now. "Tom and Mike will take care of it."

She climbed the porch steps with deliberate purpose, her hand landing on the edge of the newly installed screen door. Pausing for just a moment, she glanced at him, her voice steady but laced with finality. "You work downstairs. I'll work upstairs. Don't bother following me. Don't ask me anymore questions. Whatever this is... between you and me... it's not going to work."

Before Ryan could respond, she pulled the screen door open, stepped inside, and let it close softly behind her. Without looking back, she climbed the stairs inside the house, each step feeling heavier than the last.

Chapter 28

F aith pressed the sandpaper against the fireplace mantel, her movements slow and deliberate. The rhythmic grate of sandpaper on wood filled the otherwise quiet room, but her mind was far from her work. The antique maple mantel, with its intricate carvings, deserved care and focus, but she simply wasn't there—not mentally, at least. Her thoughts were tangled, frayed like the edges of the photograph she'd stared at for far too long this morning. Her mother's smile haunted her, both warm and alien, and the sharp contrast between the woman in the picture and the stranger who left her all those years ago gnawed at her.

Across the room, Sadie worked on one of the walls, stripping away the last bits of faded floral wallpaper. The twenty-something apprentice had endless energy and optimism, even for tasks as monotonous as this. She hummed softly to herself as she scraped, occasionally glancing over at Faith. Standing beside Sadie was Trevor, one of Faith's newer hires, whose cheerful chatter was usually non-stop.

"Hey, Faith," Sadie ventured, trying to draw her out of her brooding. "I was just telling Trevor about that new coffee shop downtown—the one with those crazy huge cinnamon rolls. Have you been yet?"

Faith didn't look up. She ran the sandpaper over a stubborn spot on the mantel, her lips pressed into a thin line. "Nope," she replied curtly.

Sadie glanced at Trevor, who raised his eyebrows in silent question. Sadie shrugged and pressed on. "You should totally try it. They've got this new maple glaze they're doing. I swear, it's life-changing."

"Uh-huh," Faith muttered, her tone flat.

Trevor, sensing Sadie's persistence wasn't working, tried his own approach. "So, Faith," he said, "you're, like, wicked good at this restoration stuff. Did you always know you wanted to work in construction? Like, as a kid?"

"Yup," Faith said, not pausing in her sanding.

Sadie mouthed an exaggerated "wow" at Trevor. Still, Trevor gave a good-natured grin and shrugged it off. The two of them exchanged a few more quiet words, their voices low, as if trying to give Faith the space she clearly needed.

The truth was, Faith wasn't trying to be rude. She just didn't have the energy to engage. Not today. Not with everything she'd discovered pressing down on her like a boulder. Normally, she'd banter with them, maybe even tease Sadie about her never-ending love affair with baked goods. But today, every word felt like an effort, every interaction too heavy to carry. Her crew didn't deserve her cold shoulder, but she couldn't bring herself to shake free from the fog she was in.

The sound of footsteps on the staircase pulled her out of her thoughts, and she turned just as Tom and Mike appeared in the doorway. Tom wiped his hands on a rag and gave her a grin that was equal parts exhaustion and pride.

"Countertops are all set downstairs," Tom said, his voice carrying the satisfaction of a job well done. "We even started putting the upper kitchen cabinets in. Ryan pitched in, too, which was helpful." He chuckled and shook his head. "But anyway, we're wrapping up. Long day, and it's quittin' time."

Sadie and Trevor both perked up at the mention of calling it a day. "Finally," Trevor said. "I thought we'd be here until midnight."

"Not on my watch," Tom said, clapping him on the shoulder. "You two go on home. You've earned it."

Sadie hesitated. "Faith? I can stay and help if—"

"Go," Faith said, forcing a small smile she didn't feel. "I've got it under control."

Sadie gave her a searching look, but didn't push. With a quick nod, she and Trevor gathered their tools and headed out, their voices fading as they descended the stairs.

Tom lingered for a moment longer, watching Faith with the kind of scrutiny that made her skin prickle. "You alright, Faith?"

She didn't meet his gaze. "Yeah. I'm fine. Just thinking about my dad."

Tom nodded slowly, his expression unreadable. "You've been a little off today. If something's bothering you—"

"I said I'm fine," Faith interrupted, her voice sharper than she intended. She immediately regretted it, but she didn't correct herself. Instead, she busied her hands with folding the sandpaper, her movements jerky and uneven. "Thanks for checking in, but I'm good. Really."

Tom didn't look convinced, but he didn't argue. "Alright," he said finally. "Try not to work too late, yeah?"

Faith only nodded, and Tom left with a parting glance that felt more like a question than a goodbye.

The house was quiet now, save for the faint rumble of power tools coming from downstairs. Faith stiffened, her hands clenching the edges of the mantel. Ryan was still working. She could hear him in the kitchen. The last thing she wanted was to talk to him right now. The complicated knot of feelings she had about him was far too much to handle on top of everything else.

Making up her mind, she packed up her tools quickly and slipped out of the room. She moved quietly down the stairs and through the hallway, avoiding the kitchen entirely. The last thing she needed was Ryan catching her sneaking out like a teenager trying to break curfew.

The warm evening air greeted her as she stepped outside, the crunch of gravel under her boots the only sound. She was halfway down the driveway, her sights set on her truck, when the sound of another vehicle interrupted her thoughts. A silver truck pulled in and came to a stop.

Faith hesitated, her stomach sinking as the driver's door opened, and Pastor Andrew stepped out. Dressed in jeans and a t-shirt, a tool belt in his hands, he looked more like a weekend handyman than the town's spiritual leader. He smiled when he saw her, though the expression faltered slightly when he noticed her tense posture.

"Faith," he greeted warmly, closing the door behind him. "Working late today?"

She didn't respond, just stood there, her arms crossed defensively as he approached. He stopped a few feet away, giving her space.

"I just came by to lend Ryan a hand," Andrew said, gesturing toward the house. "Had some free time tonight, so I figured, why not?"

Faith nodded stiffly, but said nothing. She continued toward her truck, intending to leave.

"It was good to see you at Easter service," he said gently. "I hope you'll come again this Sunday. I'll be preaching on God's..."

That did it. Something inside her snapped, the tightly coiled emotions she'd been holding in all day bursting free like a dam breaking under pressure. She turned on him, her eyes blazing with anger and pain. "How can you stand there and talk about church and God when the world is so cruel? When God lets people turn into monsters who ruin everything they touch?" She demanded.

Andrew blinked, clearly caught off guard, but his expression quickly softened. "Faith..." he began, his tone careful and measured. "What's going on? What's happened?"

"You want to know what's happened?" she shot back, her voice rising. "I found out that my mother wasn't just a selfish, horrible person—she was worse. She ruined lives. She destroyed herself. And God just... let it happen. So don't stand there and tell me that He's good. Don't tell me He has a plan because if this is His plan? It's terrible."

Her words hung in the air, raw and jagged. Andrew took a step closer, his gaze steady and compassionate. "Faith, I'm so sorry. I can't pretend to know how deeply this is hurting you, but I do know that blaming God for the choices your mother made won't ease that pain."

Faith laughed bitterly, the sound sharp and hollow. "You think this is just about her choices? What about my dad's? He's spent years picking up the pieces of her mess, carrying the weight of what she did. And for what? So I could be reminded every day of how broken everything is?"

Andrew paused, his expression thoughtful. "Faith, I won't sit here and tell you I have all the answers. I don't. But I do know this: God doesn't cause the brokenness in this world. People do. And the pain you're feeling? He doesn't want you to carry it alone."

Tears burned in her eyes, but she refused to let them fall. She turned away, reaching for the door handle of her truck. "I don't need a sermon right now," she said, her voice trembling.

Andrew didn't follow her, but his voice was calm as he said, "Faith, you don't have to face whatever is going on alone. Why don't you come inside the house with me, and we can sit and talk a little."

She didn't respond. She climbed into her truck, slammed the door, and gripped the steering wheel tightly, her knuckles white. The tears came then, hot and unstoppable, as she turned the truck around and drove away.

She felt completely and utterly lost.

Chapter 29

Andrew stepped into the farmhouse, the conversation with Faith lingering in his thoughts.

In the kitchen, Ryan stood with his back to him, one hand balanced on the edge of a cabinet he was positioning and the other gripping a cordless drill. His shoulders were tight with focus as he adjusted the angle, stepping back to inspect his work.

"Coming along in here," Andrew said, his easy, casual tone filling the room as he set his tool belt on the counter.

Ryan turned, his expression lightening slightly at the sight of his old friend. "Hey," he said, using the back of his hand to wipe at his damp forehead. "Wasn't expecting you tonight."

Andrew shrugged, his hands sliding into the pockets of his worn jeans. "Had some spare time. Figured I'd come lend a hand before you worked yourself into the ground."

Ryan chuckled, though the sound lacked its usual warmth. "Appreciate it. I'm almost done for the day, just trying to finish placing these cabinets for the island," he said.

"Need an extra set of hands?"

"Yeah," Ryan said, pulling a few additional screws from his pocket and gesturing toward the stack of cabinet doors leaning against the wall. "How about you help me with these cabinet doors? If you can just hold them steady while I secure each one, we'll knock these out in no time."

Andrew nodded, stepping into position. "Sure."

They worked together quietly, fastening each cabinet door into place with steady, deliberate movements.

Ryan tightened the last screw on one cabinet, stepping back to survey their progress. "Looks good," he said with a nod, his satisfaction muted but present. "One more to go, and we're done."

Andrew tilted his head, watching Ryan carefully as they moved to the next cabinet. "You're awful quiet," he said, voice low but pointed. "Everything alright?"

Ryan exhaled slowly. "I don't know," he admitted after a pause. "Just feels like something's off today."

Andrew held the cabinet door in place while Ryan started securing it. "Something... or someone?" he asked.

Ryan's fingers froze mid-drill. He lowered the tool and ran a hand through his hair. "It's Faith," he said, his voice dropping. "She was... different today. Distant. Frustrated. I don't know what I did to upset her, but clearly, I did something."

"What makes you think it was something you did?"

Ryan frowned, stepping back to examine his work. "Because she shut me out, Andrew. She barely looked at me today. When I tried to talk to her this morning, she gave me cold, clipped responses. And then she..." He hesitated, remembering the way she'd brushed him off on the porch earlier. "She said whatever's between us isn't going to work."

Andrew let out a low whistle. "That's... direct."

"Yeah," Ryan muttered, his jaw tightening. "I can't shake the feeling that I've done something wrong. I've been replaying every conversation we've had, trying to figure it out. Did I push too hard? Did she feel pressured by something I said? I don't know, Andrew. And it's driving me crazy."

Andrew waited a moment before responding, his voice measured and calm. "I actually ran into her outside before I came in," he said. "She was upset. More than upset, actually."

Ryan straightened, his full attention now locked on Andrew. "What did she say?"

Andrew hesitated, choosing his words carefully. "Some of what she said isn't mine to share—it was personal. But she's hurting, Ryan. That much is obvious. Something's weighing heavily on her."

Ryan's brows knit together in frustration. "Hurting how? What makes you think that?"

Andrew leaned against the counter, folding his arms across his chest. His expression was thoughtful, his demeanor as steady as ever. "The way she was guarding herself," he explained. "The way her voice shook when she tried to act like she was fine. And then there were the things she said to me. Ryan, whatever Faith is dealing with right now, it's not just about you. It's something deeper, something very troubling."

Ryan leaned against the island, his hands braced on the edge of the cabinets as he digested Andrew's words. His mind raced, trying to put the pieces together, but the image remained fragmented, incomplete. "You think this has something to do with her dad? Or the company?"

Andrew lifted a shoulder, his expression sympathetic but noncommittal. "Could be. Or it could be something she's been holding onto for a long time."

Ryan rubbed the back of his neck, his frustration evident. "I just hate seeing her like that. And I hate not knowing how to help."

Andrew's brow furrowed slightly as he leaned forward, his voice gentle but firm. "Ryan, maybe the best thing you can do right now is give her time. Be patient. Let her come to you when she's ready."

Ryan shook his head, a small, wry smile tugging at his lips. "Patience isn't exactly my strong suit."

Andrew chuckled. "No kidding."

Both men laughed softly, the tension in the room easing slightly. But the concern in Ryan's eyes remained, his thoughts clearly still with Faith.

"You care about her," Andrew said quietly, as much a statement as it was a question.

He nodded. "I do," he said simply. "Very much so."

Andrew regarded Ryan thoughtfully before offering a firm pat on the shoulder. "You know, Ryan, caring is a gift. Don't let anyone convince you otherwise." He shifted the conversation seamlessly, his voice warm and steady. "I heard James is back home now. How's he holding up?"

Ryan nodded, his expression softening. "Yeah, we brought him home yesterday. He seems to be doing okay."

Andrew smiled, a hint of relief in his eyes. "That's good to hear. Knowing James, the hardest part for him will probably be staying still for a while, give his body a chance to recover," he said with a small chuckle. "I think I'll stop by tomorrow. Check in on him."

"I'm sure he'd appreciate that. Did Faith say anything else earlier? Anything you might be able to share with me?"

"I'd rather not say, buddy. It just doesn't feel right to share what was said between us."

Ryan picked up his phone and scrolled through the string of text messages between him and Faith, searching for anything that might hint at what was troubling her. Nothing jumped out.

"Andrew, I hate to cut this short, but I'm going to head over to Faith's and try to get her to talk to me," he said.

Chapter 30

Monica looked up from her computer, her expression cautious at best. She stopped typing and tilted her head slightly. "Here to see Faith?"

"Yeah," Ryan replied, offering a tight-lipped smile.

Monica raised her eyebrows, leaning back in her chair, as though bracing herself for his next move. "Well," she began, "I hope you've brought protective gear. She's not in the best mood today."

Ryan let out an acknowledging chuckle, but it was strained rather than amused. "Good to know," he said, nodding. "Thanks for the heads-up, Monica."

She tilted her head toward the hallway, but not before giving him a look that seemed to say, "Good luck, buddy". He didn't need luck—well, maybe he did. Either way, he wasn't walking out without at least trying.

Ryan headed down the narrow hall. Light spilled from the open doorway of Faith's office, and he took a steadying breath as he stepped in.

She was hunched over her desk, surrounded by blueprints and notes. Her long brown hair was pulled up into a haphazard bun, a few loose strands framing her face. She didn't look up when he entered, though there was a flicker of acknowledgment in the small muscle that tightened at her jaw.

"Hey," he said, standing just inside the doorway.

Faith glanced up briefly, her hazel eyes cool and guarded, then immediately returned to mark something in the margins of a blueprint as though he weren't there at all.

"Do you want to talk about whatever's bothering you?" Ryan asked gently, stepping further into the office.

"No. Nothing's bothering me. I'm fine," she said flatly, never lifting her gaze from her work.

He frowned, watching her scribble on the blueprint. She wasn't even correcting anything—just doodling aimlessly in the margins.

"Faith," he tried again, his voice firmer this time, as he eased into the chair across from her. "What's going on?"

"I'm busy," she replied sharply, still not looking at him.

"I get that you're busy," he said, leaning forward and resting his forearms on his knees. "But there's something going on. I care about you, Faith. I can't just pretend I don't see that you're hurting."

Her pencil stilled in her hand, hovering above the paper. For a moment, he thought she might actually respond. But then she set the pencil down with exaggerated precision and met his gaze for barely a second, her expression as hard as steel.

"What part of 'I'm fine' are you not understanding, Ryan?" she snapped, her voice laced with frustration.

He flinched slightly, but held his ground. "The part where it's obvious you're not fine. Faith, I'm not trying to force you to spill your heart, but I—"

"Then don't," she interrupted, standing abruptly and knocking her chair back slightly in the process. She moved to the window, crossing her arms tightly as she stared out at the parking lot. "You don't have to try to rescue me, you know."

Ryan stood too, his patience beginning to wear thin. "This isn't about rescuing you," he said, his voice rising slightly. "It's about being there for someone I—" He stopped himself, the unsaid words hanging heavy in the air. He sighed and scrubbed a hand over his face, trying a different approach. "Look, whatever's eating at you, you don't have to face it alone. I want to be here for you, Faith. But you've got to let me in."

She turned sharply, her hazel eyes flashing with a mixture of anger and something far more vulnerable. "Let you in? Why? So you can feel good about swooping in and fixing another broken thing? Newsflash, Ryan—not everything in life is a grand renovation project."

Her words hit like a blunt force to the chest, but he stepped closer despite the sting. "This isn't about me trying to fix anything. This is about you pushing away someone who cares about you because you're scared—"

"Scared?" she echoed, laughing bitterly as she threw up her hands. "Of what, exactly?"

"Of being hurt, maybe," he said evenly, meeting her glare head-on. "Of opening up? I'm not sure, but something is bothering you."

Faith's expression faltered for a fraction of a second, but she quickly masked it with another layer of defiance. "You don't know anything about what I'm scared of," she said coldly, her voice trembling slightly around the edges.

"No, you're right, I don't," Ryan replied, his voice steady but filled with emotion. "I know that whatever is bothering you, it's not me. You're just using me as an excuse, and you're pushing me away."

She gripped the edge of her desk so tightly her knuckles went white. "You don't understand," she said quietly, the fight in her voice giving way to something more raw, more broken.

"Then help me understand," he pleaded, taking another step closer. "Faith, I don't care how messy or complicated it is. Just talk to me."

"You think it's that simple? Just talk and everything will magically get better? You don't get it, okay? You don't get what it's like to have a parent walk out on you. My mom abandoned me, and then she died and left me again. My dad's getting sicker by the day, and there's nothing I can do to stop it. And you—you're this big dreamer with your plans and your optimism, but dreams don't stop people from walking out, Ryan!"

Ryan stood frozen, her words sinking in deep. But he didn't retreat. Instead, he met her outburst with quiet resolve. "So you think I'm going to walk out of your life, too? What if I'm not like that? What if I stay?"

Faith's eyes filled with tears, but she shook her head stubbornly. "You won't. You'll say you will, but life will pull you away, eventually. Life always happens."

He reached out as if to touch her shoulder but stopped just short, his hand hovering before falling back to his side. "Faith, the only thing keeping you from finding happiness, is you," he said softly. "But you have to stop believing that everyone leaves. You have to let people in."

Her voice cracked as she turned away again, her back to him. "I can't do this, Ryan. I can't..." She exhaled shakily. "I need space. Please. Just... give me space."

His heart cracked at her words, the finality in her tone making it hard to breathe. But he nodded, his voice tight but sincere. "If that's what you need, I'll give it to you. But I'm not giving up on you, Faith."

She didn't respond, her head bowed as silent tears slipped down her cheeks.

Ryan lingered for a moment, his eyes searching for some sign, some crumb of hope. But when it didn't come, he turned and walked to the door, closing it softly behind him.

Inside the office, Faith slumped into her chair, burying her face in her hands. The sound of the door clicking shut echoed in her mind, along with Ryan's parting words. Her breaths coming unevenly, the weight of her fears pressing down on her chest.

In the hallway, Ryan paused briefly, closing his eyes and sending up a silent, desperate prayer. "God," he whispered, "help her... Help her see she doesn't have to be alone."

Chapter 31

F aith ran a hand over the back of her neck, the tension there a reminder of the restless night she'd had. As she descended the stairs outside her apartment, the crisp morning air hit her, clearing some of the fog in her mind. She started toward her truck, keys jingling in her hand, but movement on her father's porch caught her attention. He was sitting in his favorite chair, a mug of coffee resting on the arm, steam curling lazily into the air.

She paused, her truck momentarily forgotten, and turned toward the porch instead.

"Morning, Dad," she said.

"Morning, sweetheart," he replied.

"You feeling okay today?" she asked, sliding her hands into the pockets of her jeans as she came to rest against the wooden railing of the porch.

"Oh, I'm alright," he answered with a small shrug, giving her a pointed once-over. "But it looks to me like someone's running a little late this morning. Normally, you're knee-deep in work by now. Want me to call Tom and tell him you hit the snooze button for the first time in a decade?"

Faith scoffed, her chuckle dry as she shook her head. "Very funny."

James leaned back in his chair, giving her an almost imperceptible smile before his tone gentled. "Seriously, though. You alright? You're usually moving at the speed of light by now."

"I'm just not having a good morning, Dad. Running a little behind, that's all."

He nodded slowly, his face contemplative. "You wanna talk about it? Whatever's bothering you?"

"No," she said, pressing her boot against one of the porch's loose planks, just to feel the give beneath her heel. "It's just work stuff. Nothing I can't handle."

James studied her for a moment, and she could physically feel his patience stretching as he decided whether or not to push further.

"The meeting with the lawyer went well yesterday. He'll work on drawing up all the necessary papers," he said. "Do you have any idea when Ryan might have time to look over the financials?"

Faith froze for just a second, only catching herself when she realized her dad's eyes hadn't missed the delay. "Uh, no, I haven't talked to him about it yet. I completely forgot, to be honest. But I'll ask him," she said, the words stilted and awkward.

James raised an inquisitive eyebrow. "Forgot? You?"

She rolled her eyes, though her reaction lacked its usual playful spark. "Even I forget things sometimes, okay?"

"Alright, alright," James said, holding up a hand in mock surrender. But his expression remained thoughtful, and that slight twinkle of concern she'd spotted earlier resurfaced. Changing tactics, he shifted his focus. "How's the renovation coming along at Ryan's place, by the way?"

"It's going good. Really good," she said quickly. Too quickly. "Everyone's been pulling their weight, and Tom's been—well, you know Tom. He'll run a tight ship when I step back."

James frowned slightly, leaning forward. "Step back? Why would you step back?"

Faith hesitated, her jaw tightening fractionally, before she turned away from the intensity of his gaze to stare out toward the driveway. Her words, when they came, were quieter and lacked the fight she usually brought to conversations like these. "It's just for the best, Dad. I shouldn't have let my personal feelings for Ryan interfere with business."

"Faith," he said slowly, a firmness overtaking his tone that she rarely heard outside of serious talks. "You don't have to do this to yourself."

She blinked, a chill running up the back of her neck. "Do what?"

"Close yourself off from a good thing. Look, I'm not saying mixing work and personal stuff is always the best thing to do. But not everything has to be either-or." His eyes softened, and his voice gentled. "You're allowed to have something for yourself."

Faith swallowed the lump steadily rising in her throat, which threatened to give itself away if she stayed quiet too long. "This isn't about that, Dad. It's about staying professional. Staying focused on what matters."

"Sure it is." He sipped his coffee because he knew better than to press further, but his gentle smile let her know he only believed half of what she said. He leaned back again, letting the subject drop—at least for now. "You're a grown woman, Faith. I know you'll figure it out. You always do."

His complete confidence in her felt like a double-edged sword, but she forced a small smile in return. "Yeah," she managed, trying not to let her voice tremble.

James's eyes followed her as she shifted her weight, clearly ready to make her escape. "You're heading to the shop now, I take it?" he asked, though there was a knowing in his voice.

She nodded, already halfway down the porch steps. "Yeah. I've got a full day ahead."

He didn't miss the hurried tone, but he didn't call her on it either. "Alright. Be careful, kiddo. And... think about what I said, okay?"

"Love you, dad," she said, her voice barely audible as she walked toward her truck.

"Love you too, Faith."

Chapter 32

"**M**orning, Faith! How's—"

"Why is Ryan's truck parked outside?" Faith cut in, her voice sharp. Her abruptness caught Monica off guard. Faith mentally winced, but didn't correct herself.

Monica, ever watchful, set her pen down and leaned back in her chair, studying her friend. "Well," she said carefully, her words measured, "I imagine because he's here to talk to you. Faith, I know something's bothering you. You've been acting... strange these past few days."

Faith pressed her lips into a tight line. She sighed and tried for something lighthearted. "Yeah, life threw me for a loop," she admitted. "And honestly? I'm not sure what to do about it."

Monica's brow furrowed, and she tilted her head slightly, her expression softening with concern. She gestured toward the hallway. "Well, Ryan's here for you. He was already in the parking lot when I pulled in at eight," Monica said, tilting her head toward the hallway. She glanced at the clock on the wall and then back at Faith. "It's after nine now—he's been waiting for you this whole time. Maybe you should go talk to him?"

Faith shook her head, her ponytail swishing with the movement. "I'm not sure how," she muttered, the confession surprising even herself. The words came out unguarded, raw.

"You just talk," she said simply. "Faith, look, whatever it is—whatever's tearing at you—you need to get it out now, before it eats you alive. I'm serious. I've seen stress take bigger people down, and I'm not about to lose my wonderful, stubborn, unpredictable friend."

"Stubborn, huh?" she said, managing a weak smile.

Monica returned the smile, but her gaze didn't waver. "If you want to talk to me, I'm here. But Ryan?" She leaned forward slightly, emphasizing her point. "Ryan is sitting in your office right now. And from where I'm sitting, that's a pretty sure sign that he's not giving up on you or whatever's between you two."

Faith hesitated, staring down at her scuffed work boots and letting Monica's words roll over her. Finally, she gave a rueful nod. "You know, Monica, life is just one big mess after another," she muttered. Her voice was tinged with something close to defeat. "I really wish I could catch a break."

Monica offered her a look of sympathy but stayed quiet, sensing that Faith needed to put one foot in front of the other herself. After a moment, Faith exhaled deeply and headed down the hall to her office.

Ryan was leaned back slightly, his long legs stretched out in front of him in her chair at her desk. He immediately straightened when she walked in, his eyes locking on hers. Faith closed the door behind her with a quiet click and leaned against it, her arms crossed.

"Well, this is definitely different," she said, raising a brow in an attempt at levity. "Me on this side of the desk, and you in my seat."

Ryan smiled, his eyes crinkling at the corners, but his expression didn't fully match the humor in her words. His gaze briefly flicked down to the desk in front of him, where the paperwork and file folders she hadn't had the energy to put away were still scattered. Faith's stomach dropped as realization hit—as if the air suddenly felt heavier.

"Faith," Ryan said, his voice quiet but steady, "I came in today determined to go over the financials your dad wanted me to look at. But I'll take care of that later, I promise." He gestured subtly at the desk. "Right now..." He paused and met her eyes again, his intensity making her want to look away. "Tell me about your mom."

Her heart contracted, and she immediately felt red flags go up. Straightening her stance, she crossed the room and sat in the chair opposite him, forcing herself to look composed. "Did you go through things on my desk?" she asked, her voice clipped.

Ryan didn't flinch. "No," he said, calm and unshaken. "You left all of it here laying open. I walked in this morning, and when I decided I wasn't leaving until we talked, I sat down...and naturally looked down. I didn't touch a thing, Faith, but honestly? There's enough sitting out to put a few pieces together."

Faith stared at him, half-wishing she could muster her usual bravado, but her energy was too spent. She dropped her gaze briefly, her hands fidgeting in her lap. "I don't know where to start," she said finally, her voice barely above a whisper.

Ryan leaned forward slightly. "Anywhere," he said gently. "Wherever it's easiest."

She released a shaky breath, her voice halting as she began to explain everything—her searching through her father's files, the photos of her mother, the years of addiction and mistakes, and the silent sacrifices her father made to shield her from it all. Her fingers twisted together as she spoke, her composure waning with every sentence. She couldn't look at Ryan as she said it—couldn't bear to see the reaction to how messy and broken her family's story really was.

"And now," she finished, her voice raw, "I don't know what to do. Dad's been through so much already. How do I ask him about this without hurting him more? What if it's too much for him? What if I..." Her voice broke, and she stopped short, staring down at her lap. "Ryan, I don't know what to do with all this."

For a moment, there was silence. Then she felt the chair beside her scrape slightly against the floor. Ryan had moved to sit next to her. He didn't speak immediately, giving her the space to breathe and process the flood of emotions she'd just let loose.

"Faith," he said finally, his voice low and steady, "what our parents do—or have done—is not our responsibility. It's not our burden to carry." When she looked up at him, his expression was so genuine, so open, that it eased the storm inside her just a fraction. "Yes, their choices affect us. But they don't control who we are."

"It's not that simple," she said, her voice softer now, but still uncertain.

"No, it's not." Ryan nodded slowly, understanding lighting his eyes. "But I don't think it's supposed to be. If life was easy and tied up in neat little bows, we wouldn't learn, and we wouldn't grow."

Faith's voice trembled as she finally gave voice to the turmoil in her heart, her hazel eyes shimmering with unshed tears, raw and vulnerable in a way she seldom allowed herself to be.

"I just don't understand, Ryan. I don't understand why a loving God would put people on this earth who cause so much pain... or why He'd let terrible things happen in the first place," she began, her words spilling out in a relentless tide. "Why would He give me a mother—just to have her walk away like I didn't matter? Like I was some... afterthought? And then let her fall into such a dark, horrible life. A life that ended in something so awful that I can barely even think about it without feeling sick."

She paused, her breath hitching, her fingers twisting together in her lap as if trying to hold herself together. Ryan stayed quiet, his steady presence urging her to continue without interruption.

"Do you know what it feels like to find out your own mother, not some stranger, but my mother, took someone's life?" Faith's voice cracked, and she shook her head, biting back the sob lodged in her throat. "Do you know how deeply that cuts, how much it tears at me to realize that the woman who gave me life... the person who was supposed to love me more than anyone... could fall so far that she... she turned into someone capable of taking another person's life?"

Her voice broke entirely on the last word, and she swiped furiously at a tear trickling down her cheek, quickly looking away. It wasn't anger that surged in her tone now—it was heartbreak. "How do I even begin to process that, Ryan? How am I supposed to find peace when everything feels... tainted?"

Ryan leaned forward, resting his forearms on his knees, his hands loosely clasped. He took a deep breath before speaking.

"Faith," he murmured, "sometimes it feels like the weight of the world is on our shoulders, doesn't it? Like every unanswered question, every betrayal, and every dark chapter in someone else's story somehow becomes our burden to carry. I don't have all the answers. I won't lie to you and pretend this is something easy to understand—because it's not." He looked at her then, his warm eyes meeting hers with a sincerity so deep it softened the ache in her chest just a fraction.

"But I do know this: your mother's choices—her darkest moments—they're not a reflection of you. That burden you're carrying right now? It's not yours to bear. And it's not for you to fix, either."

Faith blinked, another tear slipping free despite her effort to rein it in. "Then why does it feel like it is? Like I'm connected to it somehow, like I'll never escape it?"

Ryan exhaled, sitting back slightly but keeping his eyes locked on hers. "Because you're her daughter. Because you love her—or at least, you loved the version of her you wanted to believe in." His voice softened even more as he continued. "But love, Faith... real love, the kind that God gives us, isn't about perfection. It's not about earning it or deserving it. It's about holding onto grace even when everything else falls apart."

She let out a shaky laugh, overwhelmed by the swirl of emotions writhing within her. "Grace? After everything she did? How am I even supposed to find grace for someone who abandoned me—someone who ended up destroying herself and everyone around her?"

Ryan gave her a sad, knowing smile. "Faith, grace isn't saying that what she did was okay. It's not excusing her choices. Grace is knowing that love is bigger than her mistakes—that you're bigger than her mistakes. Forgiveness doesn't mean we forget the pain. But maybe it means we learn to hand over the weight of that pain to Someone who can carry it better than we can."

She let his words hang in the air for a moment, processing their meaning but unsure how—or even whether—to embrace them. There was so much she didn't understand, and so much she wasn't ready for. But some small part of her heart, the part she kept so carefully walled off, desperately wanted to believe he was right.

"What if I can't forgive her?" she whispered.

"I believe you can forgive her, Faith," Ryan said gently, his voice steady and calm. "But forgiveness doesn't mean forgetting—it doesn't mean pretending the pain isn't real. It's about setting yourself free from the weight of her choices. Carrying this on your shoulders forever won't do you any good. It's like trying to move forward while dragging an anchor. You'll stay stuck."

Faith clenched her hands together in her lap, her gaze darting down as if she could find answers in the patterns on the floor. She didn't speak, but Ryan could see the conflict etched across her face—the way her jaw tensed, the way her fingers fidgeted nervously.

Ryan leaned forward, his tone soft but infused with quiet urgency. "Listen to me, Faith. God gave you your life to live for a reason, and I'd hate to see you spend the rest of it buried under the weight of someone else's mistakes. What your mother did—those choices she made—they don't define you unless you let them. Don't hand them that kind of power over you."

"What if I don't know how to let them go?" she asked, her voice barely a whisper. She glanced at Ryan, and for a moment, he glimpsed a vulnerability in her eyes so raw it made his chest tighten. "It feels impossible, like trying to lift something that's too heavy for me to even budge. What if I can't do it?"

Ryan exhaled slowly, his gaze steady on hers. "You don't have to do it all at once. Nobody expects you to have all the answers or fix everything right this second. But shutting down—shutting everyone out—won't make the pain any smaller. All it does is keep the people who care about you at arm's length."

Faith gave a half-hearted laugh, the sound tinged with bitterness. "People eventually leave," she muttered. "Dad and Monica are the only constants I've ever had in my life."

"I'm still here," Ryan countered matter-of-factly, his voice firm but kind. "And I'm not planning on going anywhere, no matter how hard you might try to push me away."

She stared at him as if trying to figure out whether to believe him, her hazel eyes searching his for any hint of insincerity. But she found none—only patience, compassion, and a quiet determination to stand by her, even when the ground beneath her felt like it was crumbling.

Ryan softened his tone again, leaning closer as if to close the gap between her guarded heart and his steady presence. "Faith, what your mother did—what your father did to shield you from it—it's devastating, no question about it. But you have the chance to learn from this, to take everything you've uncovered and use it to be better. To move forward, not backward. Don't let this keep you stuck. Don't let your mother's mistakes destroy your chance at happiness."

Faith bit her lip, her eyes shimmering with tears as his words sank in. His unwavering presence was both a comfort and a challenge, pressing her to confront the emotions she had spent years tamping down and locking away. Slowly, she exhaled, her voice quieter now. "I don't even know where to start, Ryan. I've been angry for so long—angry at her, and now I'm even a little angry at my father for keeping it all from me, even at God sometimes. How do I start digging my way out of all that?"

Ryan's brow furrowed as he considered her question. After a moment, he gave a small shrug, his expression understanding yet sincere. "You start small," he said simply. "Maybe it's a prayer, even if it's messy and full of doubts. Maybe it's opening up and talking to someone—your dad, Monica, even me."

He paused, letting his words settle before continuing. "But whatever you do, don't shut down. Don't build walls so high that no one can climb them to get to you. You've been through a lot, I know. But shutting out the people who care about you doesn't make you stronger—it just makes you lonely."

Faith swallowed hard, her throat tight as a tear slid down her cheek. She hastily wiped it away, nodding slightly, though her shoulders still carried the weight of someone battling emotions too big to carry alone.

"Ryan, I was awful to Pastor Andrew the other day," she admitted, her voice trembling with regret.

Ryan's expression softened, his tone steady and encouraging. "And what do you think you should do about it?"

She hesitated, glancing down at her hands before meeting his gaze. "Start with an apology," she said. "It's the least I can do."

"And maybe consider talking to Andrew about all of this," Ryan suggested gently. "He's one of the wisest people I know, and he has a way of helping people untangle things without feeling judged. If you're not ready to talk to me, Monica, or even your dad, Andrew might be the person you need."

Faith shook her head, the answer coming instinctively, sharp and final. "No, Ryan. I'm not talking to my dad about this. I don't even want him knowing I found those things in his office," she said firmly, her eyes clouded with both resolve and turmoil. "He's carried this weight for so long, done everything to protect me from the truth of who my mother really was—and for what? For me to drag it back up now and burden him with it all over again? I won't do that. I won't bring him more pain."

She paused, looking away as her voice softened, heavy with emotion. "He's finally starting to rest, to heal after being in the hospital. The last thing he needs is for me to pull him back into this storm that I'm sure he'd like to forget ever happened. I'm going to let him believe he successfully shielded me from all of it—let him have that small bit of peace. My mother's story doesn't need to haunt him anymore than it already has."

Ryan studied her, his gaze steady and thoughtful, but he didn't challenge her. Not yet. He could see the weight of her convictions, the sheer will she was exerting to keep her walls intact. But he also saw something deeper—something fragile, a part of her that desperately wanted solace yet didn't know how to reach for it.

"Faith," he said after a moment, "I get why you don't want to tell your dad that you know the truth about your mother. I do. But this thing you're carrying—it won't just disappear because you stuff it down and lock it away. It'll follow you, whether you want it to or not."

Her lips pressed into a tight line, her body visibly tensing, but Ryan kept going, his voice gentle but unrelenting. "You think you're protecting him by keeping it to yourself, and maybe you are. But what about you? What happens when the weight of it chips away at you little by little? When it starts making you question everything—your worth, your future, even the good things you have in your life?"

"I already do question my worth. My mother has chipped away at me for years, and now... after learning what her life had become... well, it's left a big crack in me. I don't even know where to start to get beyond this," she admitted finally, her voice barely above a whisper. The admission felt like defeat, but also, in a small way, like the first step toward relief.

Ryan reached out then, his hand resting lightly on hers. The gesture was simple, unassuming, but it carried with it a steady reassurance that grounded her. "You start where you're ready," he said gently. "One piece at a time, one conversation at a time. Maybe it's talking to Andrew, like I suggested. Maybe it's working through it with someone who understands this kind of loss and pain. Or maybe it's just... sitting here and letting yourself feel it, without trying to fix it all at once."

Faith swallowed hard, her vision blurring as tears threatened again. She hated crying in front of people, even Ryan, but he didn't look at her with pity—only patience and a compassion that somehow felt safe.

"It's okay not to have all the answers yet," Ryan whispered. "It's okay to take your time. Just promise me, Faith—promise me you won't keep carrying it all by yourself. You're strong, no doubt about it, but even you have limits."

Faith looked at Ryan and truly saw him—the man who had refused to walk away, even when she tried to push him out of her life. He had stayed. He had shown up for her without hesitation or judgment. He listened when she needed to talk, offered advice when she was lost, and gave her space when she wasn't ready. Through every wall she had thrown up, every rough edge she had exposed, Ryan had remained steady, unwavering. Profoundly present.

"Let's work on going over the financials together and get that report to dad first," she said. "Then, will you go with me to see Pastor Andrew?"

Ryan's lips curved into a smile, his hand giving hers a reassuring squeeze. "Absolutely. Sounds like a good plan," he said.

Chapter 33

Faith stared down at the photo in her hands, her thumb tracing the edges as if the motion could smooth over the ache in her chest. The picture captured a moment in time, her mother radiant and carefree, holding a bubbly, toddling version of herself. The juxtaposition of that happy image against the chaos of what her mother's life had spiraled into made her stomach churn.

She felt a whirlwind of emotions—anger, sadness, exhaustion—but underneath it all, there was a peculiar sense of clarity. Closing her eyes for a moment, Faith's thoughts turned to her father. What must it have been like to go through all of this alone? To carry the weight of her mother's choices, her downfall, her addictions—yet still hold on to enough hope to pay for her rehab? That act alone was proof of how much he had cared, of how deeply he had wanted her mother to find healing and redemption. And when that hope crumbled, he still bore the cost of her funeral, carrying grief silently, without burdening anyone else, least of all Faith.

She realized then the incredible strength it must have taken to keep all of that hidden, to endure it quietly while protecting her from the full brunt of the truth. It wasn't just about the sacrifices he had made; it was about the depth of the love he had for her, enough to shield her, enough to shoulder that pain alone so she wouldn't have to.

A lump formed in her throat as she reflected on the kind of man he was: resilient, determined, and unwavering. There was a lesson in his strength, not just in how he carried his burdens, but in the quiet grace with which he did it.

"You and Ryan worked really hard today on the financial report for your dad," Monica said as she stepped into her office. "Wanna talk?"

Faith glanced up, her defenses wavering at the sight of her oldest friend. Monica was warmth and practicality wrapped up in one, the kind of person who could read Faith better than anyone else. And today, thank God, she didn't come armed with the relentless cheerfulness Faith wasn't sure she could tolerate at the moment.

"Yeah," Faith said. "I need some girl time."

Monica's eyebrows lifted slightly, but she didn't make a big deal out of it. Instead, she smiled, her tone casual. "Well, lucky for you, girl, time is officially in session. Now, what's going on?"

Faith gestured toward the chair on the other side of the desk. "Pull a chair over. Sit next to me."

Monica dragged the chair over and sank into it. But as her eyes caught sight of the scattered papers and photos on the desk, her expression changed. Curiosity gave way to confusion, then a hint of unease.

"What's all this?" She asked.

Faith hesitated for a moment, gripping the photo in her hands a little tighter, before finally looking at Monica. "What do you remember about my mom?" she asked, her tone measured but not nearly as guarded as it would have been any other day.

Monica blinked, clearly thrown off by the question. Any mention of Faith's mother had been firmly off-limits since they were teenagers—an unspoken rule Monica had learned not to break. "Honestly?" she began, choosing her words carefully. "Not a lot. I don't remember much about her when we were younger. I remember she never seemed happy. She stayed in her bedroom a lot whenever I was over at your house."

She glanced at Faith, who nodded slightly, as if that answer aligned with her own memories. Monica shifted in her chair, her brow furrowed as she tried to dredge up more. "I remember more about your dad than I do about her. I remember how he used to bring snacks into the living room when we were watching movies. I remember him coming to our softball practices and games. I remember him in church every Sunday with you next to him. I remember one day your mom was there, and then she wasn't. Just like that. Gone. You told me never to bring up her name again, and... well, here we are today."

Faith nodded again, her eyes glancing at the piles of paper on the desk before resting on Monica. "Yeah. Here we are."

Monica's gaze lingered on her friend, sensing something monumental brewing beneath Faith's composed exterior. She watched as Faith picked up a newspaper clipping and slid it across the desk toward her. The headline was blunt—brutal. Monica's breath caught as her eyes scanned the words, the meaning sinking in slowly, like a bucket of cold water poured over her senses.

"Faith..." Monica's voice faltered as she looked up, her face a mix of shock and disbelief. "What is this?"

Faith didn't answer right away. Instead, she pushed more papers toward Monica—treatment facility invoices, court documents, letters, photos. As Monica hesitantly shuffled through them, trying to piece everything together, Faith leaned back in her chair, her expression resigned.

"This is the past," Faith said finally, her voice quiet but steady. "This is what my mother allowed her life to become. These are the things my dad worked so hard to bury and hide from me. I found it all by accident."

Monica's hand paused on a particularly damning document, her fingers hovering as if touching it would make the reality even more real. "I... I don't even know what to say. Faith, this is... this is heartbreaking."

"It is," Faith agreed, her tone matter-of-fact but laced with a deep, unshakable sadness. "But it's also done. My mother's gone... dead. There's no fixing this—no rewriting any of it. All that's left now is what I do with the truth."

Monica's gaze lifted to her friend, searching her face for answers. "Meaning?"

Without hesitation, Faith began gathering the papers, closing the folders one by one with deliberate movements. "I'm going to take all of this and tuck it away in a safe place," she said firmly, her eyes on her task. "And I'm never going to breathe a word of this to my dad. He doesn't need the stress right now. He doesn't need the burden of knowing that I know the truth about what my mother was."

Monica's brow furrowed deeply, her tone cautious. "But is that the right thing to do? Is it right to not—"

Faith cut her off, her voice sharp but not unkind. "For me, it is."

Monica's eyes widened slightly, but she said nothing, letting Faith continue.

"My mother made her choices, Monica, and I'm allowed to make mine. I won't let who she was—or who she became—taint who I am.

She's not here to explain herself, she's not here to make it right, and I'm not dragging my dad back into this storm just so I can ease my conscience. He doesn't need the stress. And I believe he's healed and forgiven my mother for everything she did. I believe he's at peace with it. And I'm not taking that from him."

Monica sat back in her chair, her expression a mix of understanding and unease. "But what about you, Faith? Aren't you carrying this now, alone... just like he is? Doesn't it feel like shutting the door on it might just... make it heavier later?"

Faith's lips pressed into a thin line as she considered the words. Then she exhaled slowly, some of the tension in her shoulders easing. "It might," she admitted, her voice softer now. "History has a strange way of repeating itself," Faith murmured, her voice quiet but resolute. "But there's a lesson in this—one my dad taught me without ever meaning to. He loved me enough to protect me from everything my mother did... and I love him enough to let him keep believing he succeeded."

"That's incredible," Monica said, her voice tinged with admiration. "You truly amaze me, Faith. Honestly, you're the strongest person I know."

She looked over at her friend and continued, "Ryan said something to me earlier—about not letting other people's mistakes have power over my life. And he's right. If I've learned anything from all of this, it's that I get to decide who I'm going to be. Not my mother. Not her choices. Not her mistakes."

Faith's hands rested in her lap, her thumbs tracing small, absent-minded circles against her calloused palms. Her hazel eyes, tinged with uncertainty and pain, flickered downward as if searching for answers in the faint lines of her skin. When she finally spoke, her voice was soft, carrying the weight of a confession she had long avoided.

"I think," she began hesitantly, her words uneven but sincere, "I'm starting to realize that maybe God's been there all along... even when everything felt shattered. Even in the silence. Even in the mess." Her breath hitched slightly, but she pressed on. "Maybe it's time I stop trying to carry all of this on my own. Maybe it's time I trust that I don't have to."

"My dad..." she continued, her voice thick with emotion that she fought to keep steady. "He's been through more than I can even comprehend. He's carried loss, heartbreak, burdens I didn't even know about. But somehow, his faith has never wavered. Through all of it, he's held on to something bigger than the pain, something unshakable."

She allowed herself the faintest smile. "There's a lesson in all of this—something I've been too angry, too hurt, or maybe just too scared to see. But maybe it's time to stop running from it. Maybe it's time to honor my dad's example, to find the strength he's always shown, and to trust in God the way he has. Maybe it's time to finally let go and move forward."

Monica pushed her chair back and leaned in to wrap Faith in a warm embrace. Her arms conveyed exactly what no words could—a sense of reassurance and grounding, a silent promise that, no matter how scattered Faith's world felt, she wasn't alone in piecing it back together.

Chapter 34

Faith hesitated on the porch of Andrew's parsonage, her hand tight around Ryan's as they stood in the dim glow of the porch light. Her heart pounded hard enough to echo in her ears, drowning out the distant sounds of crickets and rustling leaves. She glanced at Ryan, his reassuring presence grounding her swirling thoughts. His hazel eyes met hers, calm and steady, and he gave her a small nod—the kind that said, You've got this. I've got you.

She drew in a shaky breath and released it, looking back at the door. "Okay," she whispered, more to herself than to him. Then, before she could second-guess herself again, she raised her free hand and knocked.

It took a moment, but the familiar silhouette of Andrew appeared behind the frosted glass. When he opened the door, his face was a mixture of curiosity and surprise at seeing the two figures on his porch. Andrew was usually a picture of calm and composure, but Faith thought she saw a flicker of concern behind his reading glasses.

"Faith? Ryan? Is everything alright?" he asked, glancing between them.

Faith didn't answer right away. Instead, she took a step forward and wrapped her arms around him in a hug, so fierce, Andrew stumbled slightly, caught off guard. For a moment, he just stood there. But then, as if understanding just how much she needed the comfort, he enveloped her in a bear hug that silently communicated what he didn't yet have words for.

Faith stepped back, tears glistened in her eyes, though she blinked them away quickly. "I owe you an apology," she said earnestly, her voice trembling. "For what I said to you the other day—for how I acted. It wasn't fair. It wasn't... it wasn't right. I'm sorry."

Andrew's his face softened into the gentle, understanding expression that suited him so well. He reached out, resting a hand on her shoulder. "Faith," he said quietly, "you don't have to apologize. We all have moments when life gets the better of us. I only hope you know that my door is always open to you. No matter what."

Faith nodded, but the tears she had been holding back spilled over. Ryan stepped closer, placing an unwavering hand on her back. Not for the first time, Faith felt his presence like an anchor, keeping her from drifting too far into herself.

"Come in, both of you," Andrew said, motioning them inside. "Let's sit down. Can I get you something? Coffee? Water?"

Faith shook her head, but Andrew still moved toward the kitchen instinctively. Ryan glanced at Faith, quietly asking without words if she was ready. She gave a small nod and stepped into the warmth of Andrew's cozy living room.

The space was unassuming, but inviting. A well-worn couch sat opposite an armchair, with a sturdy coffee table between them stacked with books and what looked like stray Bible study worksheets. It wasn't grand, but it felt like solace. Safe.

Andrew returned a moment later, carrying three glasses of water, setting them on the coffee table. "Alright," he said, settling into the armchair, his expression kind but attentive. "Faith, from the way you hugged me—and the look in your eyes—my guess is this isn't just a social visit. Help me understand what's been weighing on you."

Faith hesitated, sitting on the couch next to Ryan. Her hands were in her lap, twisting together until Ryan reached over and covered them with his. The warmth of his touch steadied her, and she took a deep breath before speaking.

"It's about my mom," she said quietly, her voice barely above a whisper.

Andrew nodded slowly but said nothing, giving her the space to continue at her own pace. Faith's fingers tightened around Ryan's as she gathered the strength to continue.

"I've... I've been digging through my dad's old files," she confessed. "And I found out things about her. Things dad never told me. Things I—I think he wanted to protect me from."

Her voice cracked slightly, and Ryan's hand gave hers a reassuring squeeze. She looked at him briefly, grateful for his unwavering presence, then turned her gaze back to Andrew.

"I found out that... my mom wasn't just struggling with life. She—she fell apart completely. She was an alcoholic. She was using drugs. She went to prison. And... she did something terrible. Something unforgivable."

Her eyes shimmered again with fresh tears, and she swiped at them hastily. Andrew leaned forward slightly, his posture open, his gaze filled with quiet compassion.

"Faith," he said gently, "take your time. I'm here to listen."

Faith exhaled shakily, and the words came tumbling out like a floodgate had broken. She told him about her mother leaving, her addictions, the crime, the years her father had spent trying to shield her from all of it. She told him about her own anger—at her mother for what she had done, at her father for hiding it, at God for allowing it. The room felt heavy with her words, every syllable carrying the weight of pain and sorrow.

When she finally finished, her voice was raw, and her grip on Ryan's hand was so tight she almost felt guilty, though he never flinched. He was there, solid and steadfast, his presence a lifeline.

Andrew sat back slightly, letting a moment of silence settle over the conversation. Faith didn't feel judged—she felt seen, understood, even in her messiness. And then Andrew spoke, his voice calm and deliberate.

"What your mother did," he said gently, "sounds like it caused a great deal of pain for everyone involved, including her, I'm sure. But I want to remind you of something important: God's love isn't conditional on us getting everything right. Redemption is not about what we've done; it's about what Christ has done for us."

Faith's breath hitched slightly, her throat tight with emotion. She wasn't sure she believed that yet, but she wanted to—or at least, part of her did.

Andrew leaned a bit closer, his tone thoughtful. "There's a passage in Romans 8:28 that says, 'And we know that in all things God works for the good of those who love Him, who have been called according to His purpose.' It doesn't mean that everything that happens is good. It means that He can bring good out of even the darkest situations if we let Him."

"But how?" Faith asked, her voice breaking. "How do I let Him? I've spent so long shutting Him out... how do I even begin to trust that He's still there?"

Andrew smiled softly, leaning back in his seat. "One step at a time," he said. "Start by being honest with Him—just like you're doing with me right now. You don't need fancy words or perfect prayers. Just talk to Him. Tell him about your anger, your confusion, your hurt. He's big enough to handle it all. And when you're ready—when you feel Him nudging you—you take that next step, whatever it may be."

Faith nodded slowly, her heart still heavy but feeling, for the first time in a long time, like maybe it didn't have to carry everything on its own. Ryan gave her hand another gentle squeeze, and she turned to look at him, her eyes silently thanking him for standing beside her.

Andrew looked between the two of them, his expression warm. "Faith," he said, "can I pray with you? Just a simple prayer, asking God to meet you where you are."

Faith hesitated for the briefest moment, then nodded. "Okay," she said, her voice soft but her resolve firm.

Andrew bowed his head, and Ryan did the same, their hands still clasped. As Andrew prayed—his words weaving hope, forgiveness, grace, and healing—Faith felt a small, tentative shift within her, like a crack in her heavily fortified walls. It wasn't a grand revelation or an overwhelming rush of peace. But it was something. A beginning.

When the prayer ended, Faith squeezed Ryan's hand tightly, not yet ready to let go. "Thank you," she said quietly, looking at Andrew. "For listening. For... everything."

Andrew smiled, his eyes kind. "That's what I'm here for. And Faith? Remember, you're never alone in this world. You've got Ryan, Monica, your dad, and God."

As they left the parsonage, the warm night air wrapping around them, Faith felt lighter than she had when she arrived. The weight of her burdens was still there—but she felt a little better. I little lighter.

Ryan opened the truck door for her with a smile, and as they drove back to town, Faith allowed herself to hope—not for perfection, but for something better than she had allowed herself to imagine in a long time. For healing. For peace. For grace.

Chapter 35

Faith drummed her fingers on the edge of the truck's armrest, unable to quiet the restless energy coursing through her. She cast a glance at Ryan. His focus was steady on the road ahead, his posture relaxed, the picture of quiet patience.

"Let's go get some ice cream," Faith said, the words slipping out before she had the chance to second-guess herself.

Ryan turned his head, a smile tugging at his lips. "Ice cream?"

"Yeah." She said, a small smile curling at her lips.

Ryan chuckled, his laugh deep and easy. "Ice cream, huh? What brought this on?"

She paused, glancing out the truck window as memories swirled. "I guess I'm just not ready for tonight to end." Her voice softened with a wistful note. "When I was a kid, my dad and I had this little tradition. Every Friday night, he'd take me out for ice cream. It was our thing. I used to look forward to it all week."

"Well then," he said, "let's keep the tradition alive tonight."

He threw on his turn signal, heading down a side street that would take them to the little ice cream parlor tucked near the center of town.

When they pulled into the small parking lot of the ice cream parlor, Faith caught sight of the familiar neon sign that had been flickering for as long as she could remember.

Ryan parked the truck, jumping out and rounding the front to open her door before she had a chance to beat him to it.

"You know, I like when you open doors for me," she teased, hopping down from the cab.

"It's the southern charm in me," Ryan said, playfully gesturing for her to go ahead.

"Promise me you'll never stop doing that," Faith said, glancing over her shoulder as she walked ahead of him. There was a soft, teasing lilt to her voice, but beneath it lay something heartfelt and earnest. "I want all of it—the doors opened, the old-fashioned courting, every bit of it. Don't ever stop being that kind of man for me."

Ryan halted for a moment, his gaze fixed on her as she walked ahead, her every step a testament to the complexity that made her who she was. She was a force of nature—wildfire and resolve wrapped in one. Yet, there was a quiet, understated grace about her, a softness that balanced her strength. She was fierce, unyielding, and undeniably captivating. And in that moment, with an intensity that caught him off guard, he realized he loved every single piece of her.

The parlor was just as cozy and unpretentious as it had always been—a small space filled with rows of bright plastic chairs and walls plastered with local memorabilia. Strings of fairy lights were hung in uneven loops along the windows, giving the room a warm, youthful glow. The air was thick with the sweet smell of waffle cones and chocolate syrup.

Faith lingered in front of the counter, staring at the chalkboard menu as if it had changed in the last decade.

"So," Ryan asked, leaning casually on the counter beside her, "what's it going to be?"

"Vanilla milkshake," she said.

Ryan turned his head to look at her, deadpan but incredulous. "Vanilla?"

"What?" Faith countered, already on the defensive.

"Nothing. I guess I shouldn't be surprised. Simple. Classic. Original."

Faith narrowed her eyes, but couldn't quite suppress her growing grin. "You say that like it's a bad thing. What are you getting?"

Ryan scratched his jaw, clearly fighting back a smile. "Mint chocolate chip sundae, caramel drizzle. Go big or go home, right?"

For a moment, she stared at him, half amused, half mock-horrified. "Caramel? With mint? Are you serious right now?"

"Don't knock it 'til you've tried it."

"Pretty sure I don't have to try it to know it's wrong."

Ryan placed their order while Faith continued to rib him, but by the time they found a small table near the front, the laughter had settled into something softer, warmer. There was a quiet ease between them as they sat and let the moment breathe, the occasional scrape of spoons or slurp of a straw filling the room.

Faith ran her finger around the edge of her milkshake cup, her eyes dropping to the condensation pooling at its base. "Hey..."

Ryan's gaze lifted, steady and curious. "Yeah?"

"I'm sorry," she said. "For the other day. I shouldn't have been so hateful to you. It wasn't fair."

Ryan set his spoon down, leaning back slightly in his chair. "You don't have to apologize, Faith. I know you didn't mean it. I get it."

"But you didn't deserve that," she pressed, lifting her eyes to meet his. "I was angry and scared, but... I shouldn't have taken it out on you. You've done nothing but show up for me, even when I made it abundantly clear I didn't want you to."

Ryan smiled, his expression soft but unrelenting. "Call me stubborn."

Faith gave him the faintest hint of a smirk. "Stubborn... true... but I like it."

Ryan tilted his head, watching her thoughtfully. "Honestly," he began, "I get it. When life throws those big curveballs, all the emotions hit at once—anger, grief, fear—and sometimes, they've gotta go somewhere. It's not about being perfect, Faith. It's about letting people walk with you through the mess."

His words landed somewhere deep inside her, sinking into the cracks in her armor.

"Do you... really believe that?" she asked after a beat, her voice quieter.

"With every fiber of my being," he said firmly, his gaze unwavering.

Faith sipped what was left of her milkshake, her thoughts swirling.

"Do you think I'm doing the right thing?" she asked, her voice just above a whisper. "By not telling my dad that I know everything about my mom? That I know the truth?"

Ryan didn't answer right away. He leaned forward slightly, resting his arms on the table as he considered her words carefully.

"I think," he said slowly, "that your heart's in the right place. You're trying to protect him, just like he tried to protect you. But the truth..." He hesitated, his hazel eyes searching hers. "The truth has a way of surfacing, Faith, whether you want it to or not."

Faith's throat tightened. "You think I should tell him?"

"I think," Ryan said thoughtfully, "you should do whatever feels right to you."

"What would you do if our roles were reversed, and you found yourself in my position?"

"I think I'd probably make the same choice that you're leaning toward," Ryan said after a moment of reflection. His voice was steady, thoughtful. "I'd let it go. I wouldn't say anything to my dad. If the conversation ever naturally came up down the line, maybe I'd revisit it then. But otherwise... I think I'd honor his intentions and let him believe he succeeded in protecting me. Sometimes, that kind of grace—letting someone hold on to their peace—is the best thing we can give them."

Faith locked eyes with Ryan, her gaze steady despite the storm of emotions swirling within her. There was something grounding in the way he looked at her—calm, patient, and completely unwavering. As though, no matter what she said or did next, he would be right there, ready to meet her at her worst and her best.

Her heart, usually guarded and impenetrable, softened under the weight of his empathy. It wasn't pity or platitudes. It was something deeper, something raw and real—a kind of silent understanding she craved.

And in that moment, Faith realized something she'd been fighting against for far too long. Letting someone in wasn't so bad after all. Her heart swelling with gratitude and quiet awe. How had someone so kind, so steadfast, found his way into her life? What had she done to deserve a man like him—a man with a heart big enough to carry not only his own burdens and dreams, but to help shoulder hers as well? She couldn't help but wonder why, after all her struggles and doubts, God had chosen to bless her with someone like Ryan.

"Promise me something."

"Of course. What is it?"

"Don't stop being the person you are. Don't stop looking at me like you truly see me. Don't stop hearing me—the real me—like no one ever has before. And please... don't ever leave me. I don't think my heart could survive it."

Ryan smiled warmly and reached for her hand, but before he could say a word, Faith stood and stepped closer, her movements filled with quiet determination. She cupped his face gently in her calloused hands, her eyes shimmering with unspoken emotions, and leaned in to kiss him. It was a kiss that carried more than words ever could—a raw, poignant expression of gratitude, love, and trust.

As her lips pressed to his, tears spilled freely down her cheeks, but she made no effort to stop them. She felt undeniably safe, cherished, and wholly understood. This man—this steadfast, patient man—felt like both a blessing and a promise, and the depth of her feelings overwhelmed her in the most beautiful way. Ryan's hand came up to cradle her own, his touch tender and reassuring, grounding her in the moment as they shared a love that felt impossibly right.

She pulled back, her hands still gently cradling his face, and met his eyes with a determined softness. "One day, Ryan Dalton," she said, her voice steady and filled with quiet certainty, "I'm going to marry you."

He flashed her a warm smile, his voice steady and sure. "I have every bit of faith in the world that you will, Ms. McNeil."

Leave A Review

If you enjoyed this book, please consider leaving an honest review on Amazon or Goodreads.

Visit Our Website:

www.tarabaisden.com

Visit Our Amazon Author Page HERE

Find Us On Social Media:

Facebook

Facebook Author Page

Instagram

TikTok

Threads

BlueSky

About The Author

Tara Baisden is a Contemporary Inspirational Romance author who proudly calls the beautiful state of West Virginia her home. Nestled on a sprawling mountainous property, she is surrounded by the peace and serenity of nature. Her days are happily spent in the quiet of country life, writing heartwarming stories of love, faith, and second chances. Tara also enjoys quilting, working in her garden, tending to her beloved pets, and soaking in the beauty of her surroundings.

With deep roots in West Virginia, family is everything to Tara. One of her favorite pastimes is gathering on the front porch with loved ones, sharing stories, laughter, and enjoying the simple, meaningful moments that life offers. When she's not crafting her novels, Tara can often be found exploring the rich history of her home state, visiting local historical sites, and, of course, stopping by every bookstore she passes! Her passion for reading and discovery always fuels her next adventure.

Tara is the author of the Laurel Ridges Series of novels, which includes: Season of Hope, Finding Grace, His Perfect Plan, Love Redeemed, Snowbound Blessings, Sheltered Hearts and Restoring Faith all of which have been beloved by fans of inspirational romance. Her novels reflect her love for faith, family, and the timeless beauty of West Virginia.

Known for her sweet and clean romances, she creates characters that feel like family and settings that make readers want to visit again and again.

You can find out more about Tara and her latest releases at www.tarabaisden.com or follow her on social media for updates and behind-the-scenes glimpses of her writing process. Stay connected—you won't want to miss the heartfelt stories of love and family she has in store!

Also by Tara Baisden

About Laurel Ridge

Welcome to the fictional town of Laurel Ridge, West Virginia!

Nestled deep in the heart of the Appalachian Mountains, Laurel Ridge is a place where time slows down, allowing visitors and residents alike to enjoy life's simple pleasures. With its quaint, brick-paved streets, historic storefronts, and the ever-present backdrop of rolling hills and dense forests, Laurel Ridge is a hidden gem that attracts tourists looking for both serenity and adventure.

A Rich History

The town was founded in the early 1800s by pioneering settlers who were drawn to the fertile land and abundant natural resources of the region. Laurel Ridge began as a small logging community, relying on the towering forests that covered the surrounding mountains. The New River, one of the oldest rivers in the world, provided an essential transportation route for lumber, as well as a lifeline for the early settlers.

As the years passed, the town evolved from a logging outpost into a thriving hub for craftspeople and artisans. By the late 19th century, it had developed a reputation for its hand-crafted furniture, textiles, and pottery, all made by skilled locals. The town's proximity to the New River also made it a destination for adventurous souls seeking to kayak, fish, or hike along the riverbanks.

A Place of Renewal

Though the logging industry faded by the early 20th century, Laurel Ridge adapted to the changing times. Its natural beauty and deep connection to West Virginia's mountain heritage drew travelers from near and far, transforming it into a beloved tourist destination. Local shops, run by generations of the same families, line the town square, offering handmade goods, locally sourced foods, and, most of all, warm hospitality.

The town's signature event, the Harvest Festival, began in the 1930s, celebrating the craftsmanship, music, and traditions passed down through the generations. Each year, visitors flock to enjoy live Appalachian music, taste locally grown produce, and witness demonstrations of old-world techniques like blacksmithing and weaving.

A Town of Faith and Community

At the heart of the town stands Laurel Ridge Community Church, a small, white clapboard building with a steeple that reaches toward the sky. Built in 1876, the church has been a pillar of faith and strength for the community for over a century. Its bell, crafted by the town's original blacksmith, has been ringing on Sunday mornings ever since, calling townsfolk to worship and reminding everyone of the enduring values of faith, hope, and love.

The church's history is intertwined with the town's, serving as a refuge in difficult times and a gathering place in moments of joy. Over the years, the church has grown to include an outreach center that supports local families and tourists in need, providing everything from free meals to spiritual counseling. The church's welcoming atmosphere reflects the town's deep sense of unity and service.

A Growing Tourist Haven

Today, Laurel Ridge has grown to a population of around five thousand people, yet it has managed to retain its small-town charm. Its thriving tourist industry draws visitors year-round. Tourists can stroll through mom-and-pop shops, and dine at the beloved Martha's Diner, famous for its homemade pies and retro charm. The town square, with its white gazebo surrounded by flowering bushes, is often the site of outdoor concerts and farmers' markets, creating a sense of nostalgia and small-town pride.

For nature lovers, the New River offers breathtaking views and the thrill of adventure, whether it's fishing in its crystal blue waters or hiking along the rugged trails that weave through the wilderness. Tourists and locals alike cherish the scenic beauty, often finding peace in the simple pleasures of watching the river flow or taking in the panoramic vistas of the Appalachian Mountains.

Laurel Ridge, with its rich history, strong community spirit, and natural beauty, is more than just a tourist destination—it's a place where past and present blend seamlessly, offering everyone who visits a chance to experience the best of West Virginia's mountain heritage. You'll find that Laurel Ridge is a town that captures the heart.

Welcome to Laurel Ridge. I hope you fall in love with this charming small town and its residents.